ANOTHER DAY IN FUCKIN' PARADISE

PARTH DUBEY

Made with ♥ on the Notion Press Platform
www.notionpress.com

Contents

ABOUT THE AUTHOR

Parth Dubey, the author of "Another Day in Fuckin' Paradise," is a poet and novelist born and raised in India.

Drawing inspiration from the diverse people around him, Parth is a traveler at heart.

"Another Day in Fuckin' Paradise" is his third self-published work, following the releases of "Kathan: An Epitaph to Be Buried" and "Anvi: A Blessing to a Curse."

What Parth sees is a world of his own. All the books he has written, until now, are connected in some manner and tell a much broader story, a much darker side of mankind, where the world is not simple anymore and the enemies with guns are the ones in your head.

FOREWORD

In 'Another Day in Fuckin' Paradise,' author Parth pens down the story of a troubled young adult landing on the shores of Goa, unable to figure out his place in this unapologetically fast-paced world.

Everyone in his life moved on, and so did he, only to be haunted by the demons of the past. He allocates ten days, at the end of which he would sleep in an everlasting slumber, never to be touched by troubled thoughts again.

However, things rarely go as planned, and once the curtains drop, the show must always go on. Will this young adult's life end, or will the story continue?

Parth has addressed the issues that many teenagers and young adults face nowadays, considering the fact that there is no physical war anymore, but everyone faces a fight with their own self, alienated from the empathy that the company provides.

Preface

I had one question when I wrote this book: "Why do we live when death is the easy way out?"

I wondered why people are struggling to survive in a world sacrifices need to be proven and love is elusive?.

"Of course, there is always something to do," I used to think. But, somewhere, I'm not satisfied with the fact that in order to be happy, a human needs to chase some shit or the other.

I don't have answers.

"Another Day in Fuckin' Paradise" is the first step towards an answer.

Acknowledgements

I would like to thank all the people who have contributed to the creation of this book, giving me inspiration in the form of their emotions and expressing their vulnerabilities to me.

I want to thank Goa. I'm grateful to the readers who continue to support me with their valuable input and are watching me develop as an author and a poet.

Also, thanks to Anisha Pandey for the book's cover!

I
February 29

"You have to go through the cascade of my memories to get over me. Death is futile if you've yet to live; much to see," the text bubble popped up on Priyesh's phone, like ripples created by a stone thrown towards the sea, in hopes of covering a profound distance.

"It doesn't fucking matter. I've decided," Priyesh thought out loud.

"You've decided?" Bobo asked.

"Oh yes, book me a dorm bed for the next ten days. After that, I have some other plans," Priyesh replied, shaking his right leg up and down rapidly, wiping a few drops of sweat from his forehead using the sleeves of his shirt.

"Welcome to Goa! You're now part of our family for the next ten days!" Bobo exclaimed, standing up from her office chair—an age-old relic of slavery.

Priyesh had long marked February 29—the day he'd let his weathered soul rest.

The decision was the result of the multiplying sadness that exists in Priyesh's mind, like those increasing numbers of mosquitoes gossiping above your head when the sun sets and you're sitting in a park, wondering if everything you've experienced to a certain point was a dream or a facade.

"I wonder how it would feel to be finally free. Will my loved ones reminisce about my smiling face once I've gotten rid of this body?" Priyesh thought to himself, still shaking his right leg up and down, like a piston.

For Priyesh, it was not easy. It isn't for anyone. Death, the name of a tragedy called life?

Priyesh came to Goa a few hours ago. While the heat was unbearable, his previous commitment of spending his final days in a hostel in Goa forced his hand.

The wind was slow but cool. Priyesh had arrived at the airport a while earlier, renting a two-wheeler for the duration of his stay.

"I am taking this one," said Priyesh while pointing to a yellow machine on two wheels with a shabby seat that would bring him and his luggage to the hostel.

"There is a deposit. If you damage it, we need it as security," said the owner.

"Sure," said Priyesh.

"I won't get it back, but you won't get your scooty either," Priyesh thought as a smirk manifested on his face.

***

"Finally, I've reached it," said Priyesh out loud while looking at the giant building in front of him and an endless staircase leading to rooms.

"Oh fuck! So many stairs? I don't want to spend my last days moving up and down this idiotic climb. A dead body with prominent calf muscles," he thought.

The climb to the reception seemed endless for a weary traveler. A gradual increase in elevation unveiled rooms all around with dimly lit yellow bulbs glowing—hung upside down—in front of the freshly painted doors.

There was a pool as well, but it wasn't operational.

"Pool timings from morning eight," Priyesh read from a notice board.

While climbing the few remaining steps, the traveler saw a common area, but the reception was yet to pop up.

Priyesh saw a person in a red shirt with a cigarette fastened between his right ear and head. He quickly decided to reach out to him.

"Where might one find the reception?" Priyesh asked.

"There," said the man, smiling.

"Your tone, it sounds familiar. Are you from the Northeast, by any chance?" Priyesh questioned.

"Yes, sir! I come from Assam," said the man.

"What do you do here? Work?" Priyesh further asked.

"Yes, sir! I do cleaning here," the man added in a calm, soothing voice.

"Thanks," Priyesh said, ending his brief encounter in a maroon—yeah, it was a maroon shirt. Maybe red.

After walking for a minute, Priyesh eventually met Bobo at the reception.

"Hi!" greeted Bobo while Priyesh sat down on a chair with a smile.

What happened to round faces? You don't see them around anymore. I think that what people desire manifests itself in society.

Some idiot must've once said, "I do not like those round faces; I prefer sharp, chiseled faces." The others must've agreed to look cool, and now here we are: experiencing a shortage of beautiful round and brown faces.

Bobo had one of those faces—the round ones I talked in depth about. A ring curled up her nose, Bobo greeted the painter with a nice and complete smile.

"How long would you stay?" Bobo asked while repositioning her nose ring.

Priyesh was unsure.

"You've decided?" Bobo asked.

***

"I've made a 10-day booking, Priyesh; you can let me know what's up after that," Bobo said, looking into her computer's screen.

"You play songs from years ago," blurted Priyesh as he picked up his bags, headinng towards the dorm.

"And you, sir, seem like the artistic type—the ones who portray themselves to be the saddest of the whole wide bunch. Maybe just color a few strands of your hair and pick up a brush and a palette," Bobo suggested.

"You've got a keen eye, I see," said Priyesh with a smirk. "I paint every now and then. But life isn't kind to everyone. People often don't get to pursue what they want."

A moment of pause took over as the two stole eyes from each other—hiding what they hid even from themselves—the number of dreams they had brutally murdered in cold, dark nights.

"Maybe I never wanted to be an artist enough?" Priyesh wondered. "Maybe art is a hobby and not everything for me."

"It isn't easy, I know. I left my home in Kolkata a few years ago and have never looked back since. What I'm doing here—right now—this is the only thing that I know how to do or that makes sense. Feed yourself or be an artist; there's no way in-between," said Bobo, masking her frustration with a forced smile. "To go all in, you need courage."

"Wasn't Bengal famous for its art and culture?" Priyesh asked, shifting his luggage from the right hand to the left. "Always thought that if shit doesn't work out for me in

North or South India, I would go to Kolkata to sell my art."

"The city you have romanticized, that's dead, bro. The shitty mentality, the corrupt brain, and the corporate greed destroyed whatever artists were left. Those who could leave, left the country eventually," Bobo added. "So, changing the topic, I've given you a four-bed dorm at the top of the property. Works for you?"

"Anything works for me," Priyesh replied.

"I paint too, you know," said Bobo. "Sometimes, when I'm sad or feel lonely, painting is all that comes to mind."

"Same for me! I came here to paint my last canvas, which I have yet to buy," interrupted Priyesh.

"Last canvas?" asked Bobo.

"It is a long story. I am too tired," replied Priyesh.

"Well, then The Hostel will be lucky to see your last artwork. I hope we get to see it soon! Now, take some rest. You can go with the guy standing right behind you, and he'll show you your room," Bobo said while shaking the traveler's hands. "Once again, welcome to the family!"

"Family?" questioned Nitin, the kitchen manager, intrigued by the presence of the new guest.

"Yeah, he's booked a bed for 10 days, so that makes him a long-staying guest!" Bobo replied while extending her arms way above her head.

"So, you've been listening, huh?" Bobo asked as Priyesh went past the swimming pool, haunted by the screams of the people that played inside it earlier.

"You should tell Priyesh that you sketch too," Bobo told Nitin.

"That was a long time ago, and now I don't do sketches. It was a hobby—a pastime of sorts," Nitin replied, using the index finger to adjust his spectacles—his head down, voice low, and dreams broken.

***

Priyesh entered the dorm, stuffed his bag in a cupboard, and immediately went to the balcony to light up his cigarette.

Inside his jacket's pocket was a cigarette box, from which one came out.

"FUCK!" Priyesh thought. "The key to the scooty—where is it?"

After trying to give a fuck for a while, Priyesh forgot about the keys and took out his lighter to ignite his cigarette.

In the first attempt, the lighter didn't work. After a few subsequent trials, a small flame protruded out—as if a roach were coming out from underneath the refrigerator, looking for a way towards filth.

Finally, the cigarette was lit, and satisfaction returned to the painter's face as he sat on a small, uncomfortable chair that had no cushion or backrest.

From the balcony, Priyesh could see the reception alongside the hostel's own cafe. Bobo was engaged in some conversation with a man in spectacles while the man in the maroon—or red—shirt was replacing the empty water tankers on dispensers.

The slow music atmosphere of The Hostel seemed like a stark contrast to what Goa, according to Priyesh, was famous for. Not a single guest was visible.

"Why did I come here? That too in my final days," Priyesh questioned, inhaling the cigarette.

Priyesh's phone vibrated.

"Today is the 19th. You still have time to change the decision," Anvi's text said, which Priyesh ignored, shoving his phone deep inside his pockets as he continued smoking.

"When did I become a left-handed smoker?" Priyesh wondered as he dusted the burnt-out ashes from the cigarette stick, which dissipated mid-air.

The fumes from the cigarette that Priyesh held left a burning sensation, finding their way into the nostrils.

Smoke feels euphoric once inside the lungs but burns the nose when away from the mouth—toxic fumes and their noxious relationship with the smoker.

***

Looking from the balcony of his four-bed dorm, Priyesh was thinking about Anvi—the one that got away.

During the course of their relationship, Priyesh had tried to explain his situation to Anvi, who always tried to pull Priyesh out of his decision to end his life.

But what good is advice when the mind finds peace in melancholy?

"February 29—that's the day it will all be clear," Priyesh told Anvi before coming to Goa.

"I'm done trying to make you understand! I have my own shit too, and I've been fighting it alone for years! Do you even know how I feel? I have suffered because of my father, and you know that! When I used to tell him that I was being touched, harassed, or groped, he used to laugh it off. Yet, here you are, with all your 'big problems' and your irrational melancholy, which I never fucking understood in the first place," a frustrated Anvi once said.

"You have these layers to your trauma. They're too hard to comprehend," Priyesh replied.

"Are you an idiot? I don't want you to tend to my scars, but just don't say that 'maybe' I should fucking die with you." Anvi replied, using her fingers for the air quotes.

If Anvi was using air quotes while talking to you—you're fucked. Priyesh knew he was fucked.

"I can't help but be this way, and I want you by my side always," Priyesh replied. "This is a little selfish of me, but I don't know how to explain this to you."

"You want me to watch you die or die with you? What kind of twisted fantasy are you living in? I have a sister being forcefully married, a father who fucked my life up and is dead, and a stubborn mother being leeched off by my uncle. Instead of taking care of the mess I am in, you want me to drop everything and stop you from convincing yourself that you want to die?" an agitated Anvi said.

The conversations faded in the background once the cigarette burned out and the effects wore off. The high lasted a moment, but it was monumental for Priyesh, who has always believed in being chased away by the fire instead of putting it out.

"Why no, how did I end up here? Anvi used to say that this sadness inside my head is a consequence of my unfulfilled desires. But I don't have any desire. Maybe I just like the comfort that this melancholy brings me," Priyesh contemplated.

He had planned his execution to perfection. For the next ten days, he decided to sleep peacefully, eat whatever he wanted, masturbate, and drink beer and whiskey.

Priyesh felt in control of his death, which meant that he was in control of the remaining number of days that he had to live.

It was plain and simple mathematics for Priyesh—not as much for the writer penning down the painter's story.

"I finally understand. I was never in control, but now I am," the artist said. "Spent years begging people for kindness. Now, I can finally do what I feel like!"

Priyesh proceeded to close the balcony door and switch on the room's light, wondering who else was in the dorm with him.

"I don't see any bags here! Oh, wait, there," Priyesh thought when looking at a bag on the bed that was bunked on top of his.

The room was quite nice and comfortable, with two sets of bunk beds and a cupboard. Inside the cupboard was a safe where one would keep the valuables that they brought with them.

Two of the four beds were occupied, and the third one now belonged to Priyesh for the next ten days.

***

At night, Goa metamorphoses. Winds turn cold, people drink more, and the noise of waves embracing rocks starts to invite some while haunting others.

An amazing heritage, countless memories, and innumerable love stories were birthed and ended here—etched in the sand that lay peacefully, be it night or day, awaiting for the characters to return and reminisce about the good times.

"Well, I think my dormmates have gone out," Priyesh thought. "Who would like to go out at such a time? They'll probably return when I'm asleep and then disturb my deep slumber! I'll just shove my head under the blanket and pretend to hear nothing!"

Priyesh sat on his bed, with the moment of contact between the mattress and his body accompanied by a sigh. He couldn't decide which side he needed to sleep on—the left or right.

"Let's call it a hunch and sleep on the right," Priyesh thought.

A few seconds later, he could hear footsteps coming towards his dorm room, and he realized that one of his dorm mates had arrived.

He immediately pushed his blanket aside and went inside the bathroom, trying to avoid contact with the person. He could hear the door open, and the other person was on call with possibly his mother, telling her that he'd leave the next evening for Mumbai.

Priyesh eagerly waited for the person to go to sleep. Having forgotten his phone on the bed, he was now bored.

The painter looked around for some entertainment inside the washroom, but the constant tip-taps from the leaking shower irritated him.

Taking a few steps forward, Priyesh stood in front of the washbasin and turned around—resting his back on a marble structure that was integrated into the fancy setup.

"All this just to brush the teeth," Priyesh wondered while looking at the water dripping from the shower.

"Let me fix you!" Priyesh said out loud.

The soldier had a mission—to fix the shower.

Priyesh turned the handle of the shower slightly to the left, then to the right, trying to figure out the perfect spot where the leaking would stop.

"No good," thought Priyesh and proceeded to climb atop the washbasin, which was drilled into the wall and was placed on a wooden cabinet, hiding the geyser underneath.

With his right leg on top of the basin and his left one touching the ground, Priyesh found some support for his climb.

"What do you plan to accomplish here, Priyesh?" the painter questioned himself. "Maybe control?"

He extended his right arm towards the shower cap and tried to tighten the cover so that the droplets stopped coming down. His legs were shaking from all the strain.

"If you're afraid of falling in the bathroom, how do you plan on killing yourself?" Priyesh questioned his motive.

After a few minutes of wasted human efforts, Priyesh decided to come down.

Priyesh heard a knock on the bathroom door. He was flabbergasted, and his heartbeat went up. Anxious and angry because he had to face another human, Priyesh used the flush and opened the door.

"Hi bro," said Om, a fellow guest from Mumbai. "It seems like you are having some bowel movement troubles. I could hear your grunts inside. Just wanted to check in if you're okay."

Priyesh was visibly upset with the comment but said, "Yeah, I'm good."

You must know by now—the painter is not good with jokes, unlike the writer.

"This is my first solo trip outside Mumbai. I came just this morning," Om stated.

"I arrived an hour ago," Priyesh said. "I'm extremely tired from the journey. Instead of taking a cab from the airport, I took a scooty because in Goa, the rates of the cabs are higher than most people on weed.

"Considering the petrol and the comfort, the cab might've been better," said Om.

"Well, once my ten days end, who'd care?" Priyesh replied.

"Meaning?" Om asked.

"Oh, nothing. Maybe I'm just too worn out to speak sensibly," Priyesh said.

"Well, I just happened to have gone through a breakup in a five-year relationship. So, I thought that maybe I should just chill out in Goa and find some other girl," Om narrated.

"How did that go for you?" said an irritated Priyesh.

"I did find a girl in the club today, and she asked me to treat her to a drink, but I didn't have any money; I'm still a student. However, she still stuck with me after I bought her cigarettes the entire night," Om added.

"So, you basically just went to the club to get yourself duped?" Priyesh questioned.

"Nah, the girl was sweet. You see this band I'm wearing? She asked me where I got it and wanted me to gift it to her. I refused because this is personal, but I have more. So, I told her to meet me in the very club we met today by the end of the night, and I'll give the band," Om stated.

"And?" Priyesh asked.

"Dude, you really don't know about women. When a woman asks from you, she really likes you and expects some shit from you. It is common knowledge," said Om.

"What is the guarantee that she'll meet you there? Maybe she was just drunk, and she'd forget all about you once the alcohol wears off," Priyesh added.

"You don't get the point, do you? It doesn't matter if she forgets about me. I mean, I will feel bad, but that doesn't mean I don't cherish the hug she gave me today or the time she spent laughing in my arms," Om explained.

Priyesh couldn't figure out if Om was stupid or just naive.

"What about you, though? Have a girl?" Om asked.

"I have a ghost of a girl haunting me via texts," Priyesh said.

"Well, then, she's a gem if she's constantly texting. Keep her!" Om said.

"Yeah. Okay, then, I'll talk to you later, because I need to sleep now," a pissed-off Priyesh said while extending his arm for a handshake.

"Sure, mate! Have a good night. I'll be going back to the club after I find the extra band in my bag that I purchased from the beach market in the morning," Om replied. "I'll update you with the events of the night in the morning."

"Too many details, man. I'm saying it again, too many details," Priyesh replied while once again hiding underneath his blanket.

Om fetched his bag from his upper bed on the adjacent bunker and began the hunt for the wristband. He held the bag with his left hand while shoving his right hand inside the dark abyss that existed inside the bag's zipper.

After a minute of searching, Om found the band and decided to head for the door. Priyesh had closed his eyes, leaving no room for contact.

The phone vibrated in Priyesh's pants once again. It was Anvi. He opened the text from within the blanket and was about to read it until Om barged into the room again.

"I forgot my phone, haha!" Om said while once again leaving the room, closing the door behind him almost immediately.

Priyesh continued reading the text.

You don't have a purpose,
I understand.

You find sadness comforting—
Have your death planned.
Here, take my hand,
Get out of this quicksand.

The tapestry of melancholy,
Might be the home you seek.
The light of hope, so blue,

Might have lost its way coming to you.

But in a land,
Where countless stories stand—
Where the sky is huge and water is salty,
Where you can find your—
Peace and push through the melancholy,
Realizing that life is worth living for.

Priyesh disregarded the message and went to sleep, certain about his plans for February 29th.

II
Miss Mary

Lying flat on his stomach, his right hand dangling from the edge of his bunk bed, Priyesh was sound asleep, unbothered by the loud music coming from the beaches nearby or the hubbub of an excited crowd dancing under the moonlight.

At around 1 AM in the night, the door of his four-bed dorm opened, and it was Om. The slight disturbance opened the painter's eyes, but he kept his face covered with the blanket.

Priyesh took a peek at the person entering the dorm. Upon realizing it was Om, he decided to fake sleep.

"Priyesh?" Om whispered while receiving no reply from his dormmate. Om opened one of the lights in the room, deliberately, I would say.

The boy was walking back and forth, taking quick steps. Priyesh concluded that the fellow traveler was upset for some reason.

Om went to the bathroom for a few minutes. Gossip intrigued Priyesh, but he refrained from poking an agitated person.

Priyesh closed his eyes, gradually falling to sleep once again, while Om returned from his short trip to the bathroom and climbed in his bed, scrolling social media, then dozing off.

***

At around 3 in the morning, a woman entered the room with a suitcase that was much heavier than it looked—like a boulder, making instant coffee powder of anyone it would land on.

Priyesh was not a sound sleeper. A single sound would wake him up. The lady landed with a thud and closed the door with a bang, waking Priyesh up.

"Hi!" Marilyn said as a half-awake Priyesh looked at her with barely open eyes.

He didn't think much about the moment and went to sleep again while giving off a smile. Marilyn rushed to the washroom after somehow pushing her suitcase close to the bed.

"Who's she?" Priyesh wondered as his half-asleep mind gradually lost its haziness.

He opened his eyes, suppressing the movement of his body right when Marilyn went inside the washroom to take a hot shower and sleep after her long flight.

There was another guy, Karn, present in the room, right atop Priyesh's bed.

"When did he come?" Priyesh wondered.

"Great! Another dorm with only men," Marilyn thought to herself, smelling like roses as she walked out of the bathroom—looking at the lifeless bodies of Karn, Priyesh, and Om.

"What wouldn't I do to see some women in this country!" Marilyn exclaimed.

Priyesh moved around in his bed a bit, aiming to take a better peek at Marilyn. On the other hand, the lady's long flight and recent shower made her tired and sleepy.

Marilyn sat down on her bed, running some kind of lotion on her skin. Moments later, Om started snoring—loudly.

"Oh man," Marilyn thought, waving her arms around in anxiety. "Fuck! but I guess it's just another day in paradise!"

Priyesh continued moving around in his bed, trying to take a peek at the open suitcase that the foreigner had brought.

Marilyn knew. She shut off her bag and closed her bed's curtain, further attracting Priyesh's interest.

***

A few hours passed by, and the sun came to greet the residents of Goa, situated along the Arabian Sea.

You might find a church in one corner, along with a Hindu temple not far down the road. The beautiful structures stood upright, withstanding the test of time and rains.

The streets were gradually once again occupied by colorful vehicles, cars, motorbikes, and cycles, accompanied by persistent honking. Sometimes, being in India can feel like being placed in a cage to referee a fight between two giant cocks.

Karn woke up first, running to the washroom. Priyesh woke up as well. Within a minute, he realized where he was, what he was about to do, what had transpired, and where he was headed.

"It didn't have to be so, man! Why did it all have to be so goddamn complex? Life should've been fucking fun," Priyesh wondered, tilting towards the wall, while his head was still shoved inside the blanket.

Priyesh was a painter by profession and unable to sell very well. While he did create paintings worth every penny he charged, people don't love art the way they used to. Also, he refused to reduce the price of his artwork.

According to Priyesh, if an artist undermines the price of his own work, the world would never hold his work in high regard and would try to bargain for the price of bits of soul that the artist has etched on the canvas' surface.

***

Karn came out of the washroom. The clock was ticking. Priyesh was back from his dreamy world and immediately ran inside, leaving Om behind, who scrolled social media on his smartphone.

"Damn! I missed my chance," thought Om and immediately dropped down to the floor, running towards the restroom for access to another washroom—if possible.

Moments later, Priyesh came out and saw Karn getting ready for a trip outside.

"Would you like to go to the beach?" Karn asked. "It'll be fun. I came here yesterday, and since then, I have been trying to find friends, but nobody seems interested in socializing."

"Well, I like to travel alone. In the current state, I'm not looking for friends," Priyesh stated clearly. "I have to find the subject for my last canvas, and for that, I need to be left alone. I have just ten days to complete the artwork."

"As you wish," Karn replied. "I'm leaving tonight. Let me know if you change your mind."

"Fine," Priyesh, frustrated by the constant disturbance from his dormmate, coldly retorted.

"What kind of art do you do, sir?" asked Karn while tying his shoes. "Do you carry some with you? I'd love to see some of your work."

"Sure," a slightly ecstatic Priyesh said while immediately trudging through stuff for unsold artwork.

"Here, take this one," said Priyesh while handing out a painting. "I painted this with a knife, and you can keep it. There's a pretty story behind it. It was my first painting, you know, after which I decided I had to become a painter."

"Why the fuck would you give me your first painting?" Karn asked. "Won't you miss it when it is gone?"

"I don't know. I know I would be hurt, but I kind of want to be hurt?" Priyesh said.

"That is a dangerous area you are in—liking to torment one's own soul for the sake of self-pity or self-established high ground. That is not a good thing," said Karn.

"What? Are you some kind of therapist?" Priyesh questioned.

"Naah," said Karn, while taking a look at the painting.

It was a girl's face, sculpted using a knife on a sheet of cardboard. A sharply defined, oval-ish structure, painted on a dark green background with yellow signifying the feminine features of the face and white for the nasal area.

"The black hair," said Karn. "It seems like color was poured on the knife and smudged through the head—melting everything into one with a dark green background."

Red and orange were used to portray the sleek neck of the girl—the orange part symbolizing the region in front of the larynx and the red signifying the mass surrounding the hollow tube.

"How come when I look at this painting, I immediately know it's a girl? I mean, it could be a boy as well, but the face, despite having no eyes or a structured nose or facial features—just screams to you that 'I am a girl.'" Karn added.

"The truth is, I don't know," Priyesh replied. "Actually, I created this painting when I was in college, was alone, and didn't have the resources that I have now—no canvas, no brushes, and limited paint. It was my birthday, and I was all alone and betrayed in love. The girl I thought this painting would represent wasn't the one I could carry all my life. I made this painting to give justice to my feelings for that girl. This is how I saw her."

"Why were you making this painting on your birthday?" Karn asked.

"Some people... they are born to be neglected. They are born to fade into the background, into the past—mixed with muddied waters to soak the plants. Maybe I was one of them. My 24 years of life taught me a lot," said Priyesh.

"You're 24? That is such a young age," exclaimed Karn.

"I know!" said Priyesh.

"You're going to do good," said Karn while taking the artwork, keeping it carefully in his bag. "Thank you for this strange token of friendship."

"Guy's a bum," said Priyesh, dropping down on his bed with force—happy that there is one person less in the room.

***

Om had been bubbling with excitement to describe how his night went.

"So, would you like to know the events from last night?" Om asked.

"Sure!" Priyesh replied.

"I met the girl; I gave her the bracelet, and... that's it!" Om said while bursting with laughter—a forced one.

"That's it? Kind of sad, don't you think?" Priyesh questioned.

"That is how the world works, my friend. Life sucks, and then, blackouts! What can you do? You can't end it, can you?" Om added.

"You definitely can!" Priyesh reminded himself.

"I'm leaving tonight. Would you like to go to the beach with me?" asked Om.

"I'm going to tell you the same thing I told Karn: I like traveling alone. I don't like company, not in the state of mind I'm currently in," said Priyesh.

"Are you depressed or pretending to be?" Om questioned.

"What do you mean by that? Some people like to be alone." Priyesh asserted.

"As you say, my friend," Om added while taking his leave.

Priyesh once again sat on his bed, wondering about the subject for his last canvas.

Marilyn woke up, cursing the people conversing while she tried to complete her much-needed sleep.

Priyesh went outside the room to have a smoke, unwavering on his commitment to quit breathing in ten days.

"So, how should I do it? Drive my two-wheeler at full throttle into the sea. I don't know how to swim. Or maybe I should put a lighter inside the fuel tank of the vehicle?" Priyesh pondered while smoking his cancer stick.

"Oh, you can kill me for sure, but it'll be a slow and painful death, and I don't have that much patience," he thought while looking at the cigarette.

After contemplating several ways to die, Priyesh finally decided to go inside the dorm and confront a pissed-off foreigner.

***

"Well, definitely Indian men," Marilyn said while speaking to a friend on the phone. "Ok, bye now; I have work to do."

"Good morning," said Marilyn, sitting on her bed with her legs dangling out.

"Good morning," replied Priyesh. "I guess we didn't let you sleep? The others wouldn't stay shut; it's not my fault, but I apologize."

"Oh no, nothing to apologize for. I was just pissed off from the long flight and also at the fact that since I wasn't sleeping anyway, I could've joined the conversation, but you all were talking in Hindi, and I didn't understand shit!"

"Well, to summarize the conversation, one of the guys fell for a stranger he met at a club here, and the other was asking about my paintings," Priyesh said.

"Oh, so you paint?" Mary asked.

"Yeah, I do," Priyesh replied.

"What do you paint?" Mary questioned.

"Whatever is worthy of it," Priyesh said. "I came to Goa in search of the subject for my last canvas, and I have ten days for it."

"Ten days?" A puzzled Marilyn asked.

"Yep," Priyesh replied.

"After multiple visits to India, I feel that despite being welcomed here, I'm still incapable of understanding what the people here go through," Marilyn said. "Oh, I forgot to ask, what's your name?"

"I'm Priyesh, and what about you?" He asked.

"Marilyn, but call me Mary because people often mispronounce my name here," she said.

"Got it. So, what brought you to India the first time?" Priyesh questioned.

"My ex-boyfriend was an Indian—now living in Barcelona. He brought me here for the first time. I used to be constantly on the road, and we were tired of long distances. Finally, we met in India after I bid adieu to

Frankfurt—my hometown. We parted ways last year, and since then, I have spent most of my time in Portugal with a guy I have grown fond of," Mary added, playing with a few strands of her blonde hair.

"That's nice," Priyesh said. "I have a question, though. Why did you say that you are incapable of understanding what Indians go through?"

"In my numerous visits to Himachal Pradesh and Delhi, I often found people who barely had money to get by, and I, being a German, had enough to spend. The cost of living here is way cheaper, the currency is way cheaper than the euro, and I feel like a spoiled brat. This one time in Himachal, a woman with a child in her arms was begging, but she didn't ask for money; she wanted food. My ex-boyfriend asked me not to entertain them, but all they wanted was food. So, I asked him how much food 100 euros would buy and bought them rations that would last them for quite a long time," Mary narrated.

Priyesh was taken aback. Why would something so trivial make the foreigner feel so much?

"I feel that I could never relate to or understand the things that people here go through just to survive and earn the basic necessities like food and clothes. I feel sad about my upbringing in a rich country while in another corner of the world, people are suffering just because they were born on a different land," Mary said, breaking down.

"This isn't new. It is quite common in India. People beg, scam, and steal—opportunities are lesser as compared to the population," Priyesh said.

"In Europe, people have the luxury of being depressed because they don't have money troubles to the extent that they don't have cash to exchange for food. The government supports them. But here? The things are way extreme and different, and everyone's an enemy," Mary added.

Priyesh was dumbfounded. It was the first time he realized how small his world actually was.

Suddenly, Mary's phone began to vibrate.

"Oh, it's time to work. I'm building my business right now, and I have to work for hours each day. No free time for the boss lady, haha!" Mary said. "I wasted a lot of time traveling and enjoying myself in my twenties, and it dawned on me one day that I had to get my shit together and work my ass off if I wanted to retire peacefully."

"Nice thought! Okay, then, I'll leave you to it. I'm going to Anjuna Beach today to check out the beauty that it offers. Maybe I'll have something or someone to paint," Priyesh said. "You could maybe join me if you can."

"Not today, but soon, surely!" Mary replied as she got up from the bed wearing her pink tank top and white shorts, extending both her arms to the side and stretching her legs.

She turned off the air conditioning and pushed the curtains apart, letting the bright sunlight swallow the room, shouting out loud:

"Another day in fucking paradise!"

Priyesh smiled, for the first time in days, watching Mary sing to herself. He sat on the floor, close to Mary's bed, wearing his shoes. His eyes stumbled on the lady's legs, and he felt... he felt something.

"A doll," the artist thought. "She looks just like that doll!"

Priyesh's phone once again vibrated. A text from Anvi read:

You have to let me go—let the sadness melt,
Feel something new, something you never felt.

You have to forgo this constant struggle,

This melancholy that you smuggle;
In and out of your soul—
It is not good for you.

Winds have emerged in your heart,
It's just the start.
Understand that no one has it easy,
Everyone feels queasy.

Face the storm,
Forget the wrong—
Stop counting the days,
Screaming is dispair,
Silence is in peace; it stays.

III

The Trash of Youth

An old couple owns this little bar about eight minutes from the beach, if you're walking, close to Anjuna Beach. A balding, old man with fragile legs sat atop a cemented structure while his wife stood beside him, watching those passing by.

"What's with the stare?" Priyesh thought as he passed them by.

"The trash of youth. Once, the Lords of the country decided that the majority of the populace should remain irrational, jumpy, emotional fools. This sentiment seeped from fathers to sons, and now, I see the trash of youth piling up—broken, broken, and belittled," said the old man, making a weird face borne out of pure disgust.

"This trash of youth had one thing in their life to look forward to, until international trips became the new trend—go to Goa, and you're gone! Fun, parties, loud vehicles, honking, foreigners with flags hoisted on their bikes, smoking joints in secluded spaces—a home for minds that don't want to be judged but judge nonetheless," the wife added.

"In our times, things were different, weren't they? All these buildings, the weather keeps getting warmer, we're fucked, is what we are," the old man said.

"Don't boil your head. We're almost done with our lives; let these trash of youth handle their decisions," the wife consoled her husband, opening a beer from the refrigerator in the bar.

***

The heat was unbearable in February. Priyesh wanted a cap for his profusely sweating head. After leaving his vehicle and helmet in the scooty, he went towards the ice cream vendor, seeking a cold delight.

"150," the vendor said.

"What? Are you fucking with me? The MRP is just 40, bro?" Priyesh said.

"So? We have to pay rent. It is expensive here. Take it or fucking leave it," said the ice cream vendor.

Priyesh was ready to pay the money until a few other travelers came in, arguing that a soul blown away by the wind told them that overcharging is banned.

"Okay, pay fifty then," the vendor said.

"Is it that easy to bargain?" Priyesh questioned himself. "It is still 10 additional profit for you, asshole."

The entrance to the beach went through numerous clubs with loud music, plenty of beers, and average seafood to offer. The painter came in shoes and was now wondering if he should've worn slippers.

"I should've worn slippers," Priyesh thought. "Oh God, you just won't stop fucking with me!"

***

"Accountability—that is what this trash of youth lacks," said the bar owner.

"Accountability? What's that?" asked the bar owner's wife.

"C'mon. It is basically owning your mistakes," said the old man.

"You never accepted that you cheated on me," the wife added.

"See, men... we do stuff like that—no matter the age. The other day, I was watching this video on social media. A man said that a lock with many keys is bullshit, but a lock with one key is humble, good, and divine," said the old man.

"Oh? Is that so?" the wife asked.

"Yeah!" added the old man.

"You know what? You're an asshole!" the wife retorted. "The trash of youth all day and every day—what were you doing in your twenties? Getting drunk and eating fish, I presume? My mother ran a bakery, and my dad drank. My sister has a boutique; her husband? He tries new businesses every day, only to fuck them up."

"Your point being?" the old man said.

The wife was visibly upset, questioning every decision she had made in her life. For a minute, the two remained silent.

"There's no point in getting angry anymore," said the bar owner. "Fix a drink, please, would you?"

***

"Water sports? Beer? Shacks?" Priyesh was ambushed with a barrage of questions by random strangers, hired to bring in more customers to the beachfront clubs.

"No, please!" Priyesh replied, turning his gaze at the large body of water in front of him. This was the first time Priyesh saw a beach, and a vivid smile stuck to his face—for a few minutes.

The sound of the waves was soon consumed by people shouting, playing football, or playing loud dubstep music, making everything worse.

The first-timer looked around for quite a while, feeling weird watching women in bikinis for the first time, up close.

Personally, I think the trash of youth is a tragedy—people are ready to die but haven't seen girls in bikinis. Fuck!

Priyesh needed a hat and then some shade from the boiling sun. He walked for a while and then stood close to a rock, wondering where he should go.

His eyes stumbled upon a bunch of rocks that were further away, hugging the waves in the right corner of the beach. He decided to move towards these rocks and maybe sit down and enjoy the hours until sunset.

Walking on the beach in shoes was a nasty affair. They would settle in the sand, making the task of bringing the legs upwards for the next step much more tedious. Bonus points if you smoke.

Priyesh continued to walk towards the rocks, dazed and confused, like a new sailor moving across the ship's deck—all he could see was the destination.

"Maybe the sunset would be the last canvas I ever paint." Priyesh thought. "I don't have much time—only ten days. Well, today's almost over, so I guess it's nine days now."

In the middle of his journey towards the rocks, Priyesh looked at his phone and saw a message from Anvi.

"Why are you trying so hard to die when all you should do is wait for it to eventually come? Your fixation on making an event occur would only drive it further away," read the message.

***

It was 2 in the afternoon. People were resting beneath colorful umbrellas, sipping their cocktails and beers, and eating their overpriced food on one of the most famous beaches in Goa.

Priyesh had pushed through the sand, avoiding the waves as they reached his shoes.

After passing several clubs, small shops, and restaurants, Priyesh reached one of the last food and beer joints at the beach—quiet, no music, empty shacks, and close to the rocks.

Before being seated, he was reminded of one thought: "I need to buy a motherfucking hat!"

He went to a nearby shop, but the owner wasn't anywhere to be found. He decided to browse through the hats, fighting off thoughts of stealing one and vanishing beneath the surface of the sea.

"But you don't know how to swim. Nice try, idiot," thought Priyesh.

A few minutes later, the shopkeeper came, skeptical of this individual's intentions.

"Can you give me this white-colored sun hat along with these sunglasses?" asked Priyesh.

The moment you'd see Priyesh, there would be no question that he is slightly overweight. But, you cannot mention this in front of him. He is an uncool painter, contrary to popular belief.

He is a simple Indian male, weighing 96 kilos and standing at 5 feet 10 inches. He didn't have an outstanding physique, but his personality screamed that he was a struggling, depressed artist on the brink of committing suicide—a no-brainer, actually!

His beard growth knew no bounds and added ten years to his age. He didn't speak much and avoided people at the beach, unlike other men who were out there looking for travelers to hang out with.

After buying the sun hat, Priyesh went towards the rocks, unaware that the cluster was home to countless crabs—not so difficult to spot.

Priyesh hopped from one rock to another, reminiscing about the months leading up to February.

***

"Why don't you understand? It is impossible for two different worlds to coalesce into one. You and I seek different things; your love for me is destructive—for me as well as yourself. I would've lent you that helping hand you seek if I knew how. My mind is constantly on the run from myself; I can't imagine a moment where I'm at peace," Anvi said while smoking a cigarette that was unevenly lit up.

She passed the cancer stick to Priyesh, who said, "It isn't like that. I don't know how to explain this to you, but I'm a mess, and everything's a little clearer when you're close to me. You're like that tree for me—the one that shades me from the heat that I generate from within me. Sometimes, I'm lost as well, like you, and I can barely shake this need to end my life."

"You're a coward, and yet you want to do the thing that requires the most courage, Priyesh. Think about it," Anvi replied as her boyfriend tried to flick the burned-out cigarette, but it fell right in front of his footwear.

Anvi put out the cigarette by stepping on it with her heels and left the room.

"How could you have done this to us? We invested so much in your education, and at the last moment, you decide to ditch your college and pursue art? People are right when they keep their children under their thumb. Did you even think about what your father would think? He cut his own stomach to provide for you, and do you even care? What kind of son are you? Learn something from your elder brother; he might not be as intelligent as you, but he learned to give up on his dream for this family's sake!" Priyesh's mother said years ago that was when he decided that all he wanted to do was paint.

"I can't be my brother, and what did he gain by giving up on his dreams? A few praises from you? Don't you see how miserable you've made him?" Priyesh replied.

"He's happy with his family, and maybe you should get married too! Once you have some responsibilities on your head, your head won't be in the clouds," the mother said.

"You know what? I wish I was never born to you. It's better that we don't talk for a while because you can't understand me and I can't seem to interpret what you seek from me," Priyesh retorted, ending the call.

Priyesh reached out via text to his best friends in college to catch up on how he'd been.

"How have you been doing, Rajesh? Is everything cool?" Priyesh questioned.

"Yeah, I recently got promoted, and now I am earning two lakhs per month. Life couldn't have been better. I got married to a beautiful lady I met in my last company, and we're expecting a baby as well. What about you? Still pursuing art? You must be a big shot now!" Rajesh said.

Priyesh saw the message but never replied. He texted another friend, "How are you doing, bro?"

"Pretty well! Although. I do have a favor to ask you. I heard that you are into art now? See, I need a person to paint my dog's asshole like the color of his coat," replied the friend, accompanied by poop and laughter emojis.

This brought a smile to Priyesh's face.

While the thoughts of jumping into the sea haunted Priyesh, he knew that the moment wasn't right. He still had nine days to paint the last painting on the canvas that he had yet to purchase.

"Is a painter defined by what he draws? Is a writer only limited to the words he writes? Does a woman's capability lie in her ability to raise a child? Is a man only good for the money he brings to the table? I never said I would take you on a cruise through the world, offer you breakfast at the top chains, or spend nights with champagne tastes," Priyesh told Anvi.

"When you were courting me, you said you would get me anything I wanted and protect me from everything dark and deep—where is that person? You didn't get me anything I wanted. In fact, you didn't give me anything; you made my life much worse with all the seepage of sadness from your personality," said Anvi.

Priyesh's legs were now tired of standing on the rock. The flashbacks were over. He decided to return to the shack, lie down, have something to drink, and watch the sun set in the next few hours.

"The cigarettes and beer are more expensive than the market rate," Priyesh argued with the restaurant manager, who also owned the shack. "It seems like you also have to pay heavy rent, huh? Get me this, this, and this. Thanks."

The manager decided to take leave.

"Wait!" said Priyesh. "The Wi-Fi password, please."

A few hours passed, and the sun lost its bright light, as if a candle were being extinguished. Priyesh was on his fourth beer can and was already inebriated. His tolerance for alcohol wasn't much, and he suffered from a severe lack of self-control.

"C'mon, just drown in the water already," Priyesh told himself, after realizing that sunset wasn't the last painting he was dreaming of.

The umbrella wasn't helpful anymore because the sun was quite close to the sea. The whitish hue turned reddish-orange; dogs, cats, and birds all had found harmony—not overstepping individual boundaries.

***

"Where are you going?" a strange man in the Delhi Metro asked Priyesh.

"To the airport," Priyesh replied.

"Vacation?" the man questioned.

"Kind of. I'm going to Goa," Priyesh replied.

"Wow!" the man said.

"Well, I'm going to the railway station. You know, this morning when I woke up, a thought came into my mind, and seeing you just solidified my conclusion," the man said.

"What thought would that be?" a curious Priyesh asked.

"Traveling is a luxury. So is the thought of making something of yourself. Meanwhile, many people have it much worse than us. Some can't walk, some are fighting mental battles, some do not have money to feed their children, and many are stuck in some situation or another. It is miserable out there, and I believe we might be the lucky ones," the man said.

"There's so much misery because there are so many of us. Why do people keep living if they're broken and broke? Why not just end life and get it over with?" Priyesh replied.

"Maybe because it is quite selfish and because death is not the solution. You just transfer your problems onto someone innocent. Wouldn't you rather be remembered as the person who tried to win over the demons that came his way, not a coward who failed to choose the path that required courage?" the man asked.

"Not as easy, man. Try being an artist in this country," said Priyesh.

"The last time I visited Goa was in 2018 with my collegemates. We drank and had a lot of fun, but at the same time, I realized that there was more to life than drinking and partying," the man said. "So I decided to cycle. I've been cycling for years—to Ladakh, Kanyakumari, and everywhere else you can think of," the man said.

"So?" Priyesh questioned.

"So do you think cycling throughout the country is easier than being an artist?" the man asked.

"Not many people would think so, and certainly not me," Priyesh replied.

"What do you do, sir?" the man interrogated.

"I'm a painter," Priyesh said.

"That's great, man! How can you say you do not have it good? Pursuing art is a luxury that people in our country can rarely afford," the man said.

"What do you know about my life that you've jumped to such a marvelous conclusion?" Priyesh asked.

"Well, I do not. But your life isn't all garbage—these brief moments, like the one between us, they make you feel special," the man explained.

"Thanks for the kind words, sir, but I believe that one moment of happiness cannot negate the existence of a life full of pain," Priyesh said as the metro stopped. "We've arrived."

"Sure. By the way, what's your name?" the man asked.

"Prashant," said Priyesh, faking his name.

"I'm Sushant," said the man, while also getting out at the same station, keeping a hand on Priyesh's shoulder, adding:

The ugliness makes beauty appear stronger,
Makes you wish happiness lasted longer.

Travel to Goa; you might change your outlook,
One fine day, you'll read your own storybook.

Realize that things weren't as bad as you made them look,
That you trying your best to live in the moment was all it took.

IV

Baga Beach

"At least you could've been loyal," Anvi whispered in Priyesh's ears, pulling him closer to her chest, suffocating him—the painter opened his eyes, gasping for air.

"Another day in fucking paradise!" Mary exclaimed while forcing the curtains of the room apart.

"Good morning, Miss Mary," Priyesh said.

"Morning!" said the foreigner.

Everything seemed to be a blur for Priyesh—the strong sunlight blinded him. Looking away from the windows, the painter saw a book in Mary's bag, "Be the Richer Dad."

"Well, all this is useless, you know. Money—these authors claim to understand the poor people's mindset; it's all bullshit," Priyesh commented.

"It is your opinion. Some people have different perspectives. You see, you aren't the only one that exists on this planet. This book has an audience—people like me." Mary replied.

"Well, if you do like to read, here's something I wrote yesterday at the Anjuna Beach," Priyesh said, handing out a piece of paper hesitantly. "Be gentle with the criticism, please!"

"Man, am I tired of people underestimating themselves! Cheer up, guy," said Mary.

Priyesh took out his phone, handing it over to Mary. "Here."

Mary took the phone and read out loud, "The strong winds befriended the sun."

"No! Please, in your mind," Priyesh said.

"Your own words make you uncomfortable?" Mary asked.

"I don't know. I just don't like hearing them. I don't know if they are any good," said Priyesh.

"Okay," Mary replied, extending the 'y' like cheese on pizza. "Here it goes! Shush now."

The strong winds befriended the Sun,
The two sought to write a story like none.

A green umbrella covers my head,
I look out to the sea and find myself instead.
Healing is a gradual process," they said.

But once you are healed,
The art remains concealed—
But are you ever healed if you broke once again?
You're losing ways to distract the heart from pain.

Don't talk to them, the voices are not allowing you to feel,
Never be afraid of emotions; bleed the blood for real.

When I talk to water, I talk to myself,
I see the water, but I look at myself.

What if this day stops moving forward—
Just me, you and the sea?
Won't you run towards the last ice cream store before it all
melts?
Oh no! I just realized,
We are all frogs stuck inside bottomless wells.
The more you buy, the more they'll sell.

Remember to look out the window every once in a while,
Remember to take a deep breath and smile.
Time's a wasted luxury, freedom is an expensive treat,
So take your pen out of your pocket,
Write what you need.

Throw your ego away—
Why did I write this poem? IDK,
Maybe feel a little, fuck a little, love a little, die each day, and;
When all's said and done, live a little each day.

"For a person suffering from chronic melancholia, this poem is fairly positive, don't you think?" Mary said.

"'IDK.' That is the poem's title," said Priyesh, taking his toothbrush out from the bag.

"I love the ice cream part and how you paint pictures with your words. Publish books, and I'll support ya!" Mary added.

"I'm already a painter—that's enough art for me," Priyesh said.

"Well, what's your age?" Mary questioned.

Priyesh went silent for a while, engaged in some complex mathematics.

"I'm 24," he concluded.

Mary burst into laughter—the sound occupying the room. Her cheeks went red, and dimples manifested.

"Can you guess my age?" Mary questioned.

"Umm, I'd say 29–30," Priyesh guessed.

"Sweet Jesus! You're a kid," Mary said, once again bursting into laughter.

"I'm no kid," Priyesh said, possibly hurt from the constant laughter. "You'll see how I shine once I'm back from the washroom!"

"Shine your teeth first," Mary retorted, once again giggling as if a child after a successful cartwheel.

***

Five minutes later, Priyesh came out of the washroom, worried.

"There is some sort of smoke coming out of the switchboard connected to the geyser. I think it was left on all night. Someone fucked up. The two other guys who left last night—Karn and Om—must be the work of those idiots," Priyesh said.

"Umm, yeah, possibly," said Mary, hiding her face from her dormmate.

"Hey! What happened?" Priyesh asked. "Why don't you come here? Should I shut off the switch?"

Mary stayed silent for a few seconds and then ran towards the washroom. "If you get this fixed, we will go to the beach today!"

"Pinky promise?" Priyesh said.

"Yeah, yeah, done!" Mary said while cackling once again. "Such a kid! Haha!"

A motivated Priyesh called the reception, and the man in red came up to fix the issue.

"This is fucked," said the man.

"Please help! See if you can do something," said Priyesh—subtly begging like the man at the mercy of a samurai, wanting his honor to be left intact in front of this foreigner he fancied.

"Cool," said the man while bringing his hand forward, opening his palm like a blossoming flower.

"Later," said Priyesh.

A few minutes passed. The man in red changed the switch. As he left the room, Priyesh bribed him with a small pack of cigarettes.

Priyesh closed the door and turned to Mary. "I did what you asked. Now, to the beach."

"I made a promise, didn't I?" Mary said. "Go; I need to work! The faster I finish, the better!"

"No!" said Priyesh with a creepy smirk.

"Don't. Please," said Mary.

Priyesh left the room.

***

Priyesh headed for the cafe, which was quite busy. He ordered lunch and sat down, watching two staff members play foosball.

"Isn't this the game where the players pretend to give a shit about football?" Priyesh chimed in.

No response came. Maybe they did not hear him.

Of the two players, one was taller and wore a sun hat and spectacles. The other was shorter, wearing a black shirt and blue jeans.

"How do you play this game?" Priyesh questioned.

"Well, it's easy, sir. You have four rods—use 'em like you dick and shoot the shot," said Kunal, the one in the black shirt, with a smirk.

"I've heard enough! Give me a spot," Priyesh said.

"Come. Play from my side. I'll defend; you eye Sid Bhai's hole," explained Kunal. bursting into laughter.

Thus began a game of skills that Priyesh didn't have.

In one corner was Sid, playing solo and blinded by the sun. Karn and Priyesh teamed up but could only score a single shot.

"Want to play another?" asked Sid.

"Excuse me?" said a woman, who came barging into the cafe. "Your staff is totally incapable and useless. They can't do one thing right! I asked them to get my room ready by 1 PM, and it's already 4:30, but they haven't done shit!"

Sid went with the lady to check on the staff.

"Do you get such guests often?" Priyesh asked.

"Yeah, well… Sid handles them. However, we are at fault in this case. But what would you expect if you pay peanuts?" said Kunal.

"True," said Priyesh. "I will score at least one goal, solo—that's a promise."

"What? In foosball?" questioned Kunal. "Haha! Sure, sure!"

Another round began.

"You're losing!" Kunal said.

There was nothing Priyesh could do. So, after a point, he just started rotating the rods rapidly.

"BOOM!" Priyesh exclaimed as the ball left the table's parameters, nearly turning a guest's eye black.

"Guys, chill out!" said the guest.

The game ended abruptly.

Kunal and Priyesh—stuck side-by-side—went to the edge of the cafe, where smoking was allowed.

The cancer stick was lit up.

"You know—this scenario would make a damn excellent painting," said Priyesh.

"Definitely!" Kunal replied.

"Wait until you see the sun setting through the cafe. But the sunsets keep getting here with each day. Each day, they get better," said Kunal while taking a deep puff from the cigarette.

"Rally?" Piyesh questioned.

"Yeah!" said Kunal, while passing the cigarette.

"In my early twenties, I used to think life was shit and everything happening was for one reason—to make breathing for me more miserable. But after a while, I have accepted that everyone is shitty; that makes me less 'shittier,' I guess?" Kunal stated.

"But," said Priyesh.

"Stop!" Kunal interrupted. "Tell me what's with the German?"

"What German?" Priyesh asked.

"The girl, brother! Is she interested?" Kunal doubled down.

Priyesh went silent.

"Goa is treating you well, I believe," Kunal said.

"You're misunderstanding. She and I are going to Baga Beach today because I got the geyser fixed," explained Priyesh.

"I bet you weren't supposed to tell that," Kunal smiled. "When are you guys leaving?"

"In the night," Priyesh replied.

"Until she arrives, eat something or have a beer," Kunal suggested.

"You're right!" said Priyesh.

"By the way, we don't serve non-veg—only eggs. So, would you like to try shakshuka with parathas? It's our best-selling dish," said Kunal.

"Cool," Priyesh agreed with a sigh.

"Also, would you like to hang out? I have a day off tomorrow. Let's go to Redi Beach," said Kunal.

The painter nodded, putting headphones in his ears and zoning out.

***

Soon, it was midnight. A cold breeze blew throughout the hostel, finding Priyesh on a corner table of the cafe, sketching with a pencil.

He drew a face. A thin one, well-defined, and possibly foreign. It was only an outline, an incomplete face created from scratch, with no past, no present, and no future. It could take days to take shape via countless coarse contacts between the pencil and the table.

"You're forgetting about me, aren't you? You're moving on, seeking a different life. It isn't about your last painting anymore, is it? Be careful; you're cursed like me—everything you care about vanishes the moment you come close to it," Anvi texted.

A faint sound of footsteps originated from a corner of the building. Mary was coming.

"The bloodiest wars were won and lost in the mind—the phoniest lay naked on the ground with their lies—you're lying to yourself," Anvi added.

"What the hell are you doing—sitting here all by yourself, in the dark?" Mary asked.

Priyesh kept his phone inside, welcoming the foreigner with a smile.

Mary sat down on the chair adjacent to Priyesh, overjoyed by the fact that her work had finished on time.

"Miss Mary, I've been waiting for you," said Priyesh, adjusting his shirt to look a little better than a homeless man and a little worse than a gentleman.

***

Miss Mary had this quaint habit of rolling the strands of her hair—like a mermaid sitting on a rock in the middle of the sea—singing a mellow tune, luring sailors towards her.

The painter could sit and watch her for hours and smile, getting lost in the mesmerizing essence of her golden lochs. Mary's smile brightened the day of the man who had sold his soul to melancholic demons.

"Let's go to the beach!" Mary said.

"I've noticed you play with your hair a lot. Why is that?" Priyesh asked.

"Oh, it's just something I do that keeps me calm and away from anxiousness. It helped me through therapy and other shit," Miss Mary said. "Let's talk about that some other time."

Priyesh took out the keys to his two-wheeler, flashing them in front of the foreigner.

It took the duo a total of 15 minutes to arrive at Baga Beach following a drive through the dimly lit and narrow roads of Goa.

During the ride, Miss Mary, hesitant to hold Priyesh's shoulders, eventually wrapped her right hand around his chest, placing her left hand on his shoulders.

She was excited.

Everyone has a thing—some might say they like mountains, some love forests, and Mary? She was a beach person.

Priyesh's heart was beating faster every time Mary's hand warmed his chest. He tried to subdue his excitement but failed as Mary's voice echoed close to his ears throughout the journey.

"I can hear the sound of the waves; it's wonderful!" said Mary, asking Priyesh to come close.

"You know, in Germany, the month of February is so bland, and everything just lacks color. People lack enthusiasm to do anything—no parties, no music, and no good food! However, the summers are better," said the traveler.

"We need to buy you a helmet," said Priyesh.

"Oh yes! You know, I saw a post on social media about a man who broke his teeth in India because he didn't have a helmet. India is a scary place to drive—a very well-known fact," said Mary.

"Sure, Miss Mary!" Priyesh replied, watching Mary do a celebratory dance to his affirmation.

She went ahead, hopping alternately on each leg—her hair bounced haphazardly. She removed her slippers, held them in her hands, and danced all the way to the beach, shouting,

"Another day in fucking paradise!"

It seemed like Mary was a kid who received the sweetest candy as a gift—the kind that left an everlasting taste. Her brown eyes shone, sparkling with happiness.

But the happiness was short-lived. The moment Mary stepped foot inside the premises of Baga Beach, chaos unfolded.

"Too many drunk people here," said Priyesh.

"And lots of loud music! I can't hear you properly. It is so late in the night, and yet they're allowed to do this? The fuck," said Mary. "People are puking anywhere!"

The duo held each others' hand and ran towards the quiet side of the beach in tandem.

"Why do you call me Miss Mary?" the foreigner asked.

"I don't know," Priyesh said.

"Well, that's a first for me!" Mary said, laughing and kicking the water from the sea. "Nobody has ever called me

Miss Mary, and I certainly don't mind, haha!"

"There you go, once again, making faces," said Mary. "Look at all this garbage here, man! People don't respect shit. Every time I visit this country, all I see is litter everywhere."

She picked up a few cans and bottles of beer, throwing them in a dustbin nearby.

***

"This is the first time I came to a beach in the night, and it is just beautiful," said Priyesh as the duo sat on the sand.

The blackness of the beach and the emotion on the painter's face were not complementing each other—their existence together was a blasphemy in the name of life.

"I hear the sound from the waves afar, but I don't see them," said Priyesh.

"Ahh! There we go with the melancholy," said Mary.

"No! I mean, it is a genuine question," said Priyesh.

"You don't see them because you are not trying. Do you have a torch? Maybe use your phone's flashlight," instructed Mary.

"It doesn't work like that," said Priyesh.

"Maybe it does? Have you tried?" Mary added.

"Fuck it! I feel hungry," said Priyesh.

"Well, there are several tables; let's take one and order," Priyesh said.

A minute later, Mary was holding a menu in her hand, seated comfortably.

"Oh man, you need to try shrimp, prawns, and some of the other stuff I'm ordering. I don't eat chicken, beef, or lamb, but seafood—I love it!" Mary said.

"Never had seafood," said Priyesh.

"Shisha?" asked Mary.

"Sure!" said Priyesh. "Anything with tobacco is welcome."

Mary proceeded to order shisha as well. The waiter took the order and then lit up a candle enclosed in a glass structure open at the top for air.

Priyesh and Mary looked at each other and smiled. The foreigner was wearing a yellow dress—her white skin was painted yellow with the flame that penetrated the glass.

"Golden hair, red lips, slight cleavage, and two beautiful dimples," Priyesh murmured.

"What?" asked Mary.

"A lot of firsts," said Priyesh.

"Like?" the German asked.

"This is the first time I am in the company of a German, the first time I'm trying seafood, and you know—never in a million years could I have thought that I would be having dinner with a German," said Priyesh.

Mary smiled, adjusting the gown that ran over her entire body and had become one with her golden lochs.

"You have melted and solidified in my mind—like that wax from the candle," said Priyesh.

"Already?" asked Mary.

"Are you a mermaid, or am I just dreaming?" Priyesh questioned.

"Ahh! Stop it now," said Mary.

The painter liked being around Mary. Her smile, her childishness, and the carefully created sculpture that was Mary's body made Priyesh feel something—a feeling that, for him, was rare.

For a while, both remained silent.

"Hey, you think a lot—I've seen that. In the dorm, here, and possibly in your home as well. C'mon, tell me, what do you keep thinking about?" Mary asked.

"Honestly? I don't know. I mean, I don't really know what to live for anymore. The only thing that keeps me alive right now is my final painting, which I have to complete in the upcoming nine days. After that? I don't really know. I don't feel like living anymore," said Priyesh.

"It feels like you have an alarm that tells you, 'I don't want to live anymore.' Get rid of this alarm, man," said Mary. "Tell me—have you traveled all of Europe? Have you seen an aurora? Have you been to the United States and seen Los Angeles? These are the things I can name right off the top of my head. If I put some more thought into it, I can prepare an endless list. How can you say that there is nothing to live for anymore?"

"Why would I want so much hassle?" Priyesh wondered.

"You're basically unmotivated, it seems," Mary concluded.

"I have a motivation—finish my last painting," said Priyesh.

"See—that's the alarm," said Mary. "There is no last of anything! It is just one after the other until it is not. Instead of drowning in melancholy, why don't you live for others?"

"What do you mean by that?" Priyesh asked.

"For example, I sponsored a child in India. I paid for her food, education, and clothing all the way until she was 18, and there are organizations that help these children. Once they turn 18, they're free to go and live their lives. I send money every now and then, make a life, and not take one," said Mary.

"That is cool, lady!" said Priyesh.

"When I get pictures of that child and her regular updates on how she's growing and living like other children, I just feel happy. I believe that people who are melancholic are just selfish. But that's me! My suggestion: come to Europe, man; it's awesome!" Mary added.

"Sister, please," a little girl came from behind, asking Mary to buy one of the glowing ribbons and bunny ears.

"No! I don't want to, sweetie," said Mary.

The girl was persistent, around 10–11 years old, and one of the cutest people on the beach. Mary was not immune to this cuteness and finally gave up—bought a rabbit ear for herself and a few glowing sticks and wristbands for the both of them.

The girl also made Mary's hair using her glowing sticks—creating a unique, messy bun.

"It looks so beautiful on you! I love it," said Priyesh.

"Click a picture of the hair. I want to see," said Mary. "Maybe I'll try putting this hairstyle together in Germany and tease my girlfriends!"

Priyesh started clicking pictures as the little girl stood by.

After a while, the little one snatched the phone from Priyesh's hands. "You definitely don't know how to take pictures."

The girl knew much more about Priyesh's phone than he did, clicking insanely beautiful pictures of the foreigner.

After spending around 3 hours at the beach, it was already 3 AM. The waiter asked the duo to leave because they had to open again by 7 AM.

The duo left the beach premises and came into the parking lot, which was empty.

Streets were abandoned by the vehicles, and no cops or tourists were bargaining. The air was calm, and the beach hooligans slept in their vomit. The shops were shut down, and food joints closed.

Mary and Priyesh—a little tipsy—made their way back into the hostel, immediately washing the sand and preparing for a good night's sleep.

Priyesh dropped on his bed and could see Mary preparing hers as well. He quietly approached the mermaid, saying, "Miss Mary, thanks for today!"

"Oh no, thank you! I had a lot of fun, and the conversations were just amazing. We're going to do this again soon, pinky promise! Also, a trivia—the mermaid is my favorite creature—it's my everything, haha. You were spot on!"

Priyesh smiled and blushed a little. "By the way, I still don't believe you're 40. You were fucking with me, right?"

"Oh, you're a baby! But I'm not forty; I'm thirty-nine!" Mary revealed.

V
Cockroach

"I used to think that you would be the one, you know?" Anvi said, moving towards a bedside table to grab a smoke.

"Know what?" asked Priyesh, lying on a dirty bed, staring at his fingers.

"Forget it," said Anvi, sparking the lighter and inhaling the smoke from the cancer stick.

"Dude! When did we break this mirror?" Priyesh asked.

"We? You broke it," said Anvi.

"I did no such thing," claimed Priyesh, hiding his face underneath a pillow.

"Fuck off," said Anvi. "Don't be cute with me now."

"I am so sorry. My tongue slipped," explained the painter.

"What about the mirror? Is your broke ass going to pay for that?" said Anvi.

"I will definitely pay for it next month," Priyesh promised.

"Guys like you—you're cockroaches, disease carriers. The sadness you bring once you enter through that door is suffocating for me 'cause I have not given up. But you have. I spent the better part of a year trying to make you understand. But you don't. I don't think I want to be with you anymore," said Anvi.

"You're just angry, Anvi. Trust me. I am a changed man. We won't fight as much from now onwards. What we're doing right now is a disagreement... the ones born from misunderstanding. You've just misunderstood me. That's right. You've just misunderstood me," said Priyesh.

"You have to go through the cascade of my memories to get over me. Death is futile if you've yet to live; there is much to see," a text popped up.

"That's bullcrap," thought Priyesh, rubbing his eyes. "Was that a dream? Or the truth? What time is it? Is it time for class? When did I sleep? Where am I? Oh yeah! I came to Goa. Oh, idiot! Anvi isn't with you anymore. There's a hot German in the adjacent bed. Wake up now!"

"Hey painter!" said Mary, waving her arms from side to side.

"Yoga?" asked Priyesh.

"Do you think you get to stay hot without effort?" Mary retorted.

"Nah! It's just that working out is hard. I don't want to," said Priyesh.

"Do you want to, maybe, fuck me?" asked Mary.

"What?" Priyesh, stunned, with his heart atop his tongue.

"You don't? Or do you?" Mary asked, now in a slightly thicker voice.

"I... I do," whispered Priyesh.

"What? What do you want to do?" Mary's voice thickened.

"I want to fuck you!" Priyesh spoke out loud.

"You want to? Couldn't hear the last part," said Mary, holding Priyesh's right hand, pulling him closer to her chest.

"I... I can't think," said Priyesh.

"You don't have to," said the German, placing her palm on the painter's cock.

"What are you..." said Priyesh but was interrupted by Mary.

"Don't talk. Just tell me. What do you want to do to me?" Mary asked, now in a calmer, more feminine, and erotic voice.

Priyesh could feel a throb on his dick as Mary's grip tightened.

"What is going on?" the painter remained unsure.

"Do you want it?" asked Mary.

"What?" mumbled Priyesh.

"My tongue, on your dick," said Mary.

"I do!" replied Priyesh.

"Then say it!" said Mary.

"What?" asked Priyesh.

"What do you want to do to me? WHAT?" Mary asked.

"I WANT TO FUCK YOU!" Priyesh shouted at the top of his lungs, unbuttoning his pants.

***

"Hey. Man! Hey, dude! Are you fine?" asked Mary.

Priyesh returned from his eccentric dream. "What?"

"You were murmuring in your dream, man! Who do you want to fuck? I mean, do you want to fuck someone literally, or are you in a fight or something?" Mary asked.

"Ah, nothing! It is all fine. Just some stupid nightmare, I guess," said Priyesh.

"Cool," said Mary. "I am going out for a while. Maybe you'd like to clean up?"

"What?" the puzzled painter asked.

"Nothing. Just look after yourself," said Mary.

"Okay, I guess," a confused painter said as the foreigner left the room.

"What is she talking about?" Priyesh thought, taking a gander inside his blanket.

"Fuck! Fuck!" exclaimed Priyesh, slapping himself thrice. "I need to apologize!"

Panic had set in. The painter's mind broke down, unable to find a way through this shithole.

A knock was heard on the door.

"She's back," thought Priyesh. "I need to clean up!"

"Open up once done," said Mary, while playing with the strands of her golden hair.

"You know, I like what you've done with this property. But you guys are expensive," Mary told a member from the cleaning staff.

The door opened. New clothes on his body. Priyesh, still panicking, greeted everyone inside.

"Please clean the beds," said Mary. "This idiot here just came."

"I have been here a while, Mary," said Priyesh.

"Oh, sorry. I mean, he just masturbated. I want his bed cleaned and this cockroach CLEANED FROM MY FUCKING ROOM," said Mary as her voice began to grow louder in the end.

The painter's heart sank. His mind went numb. It was all over... he had to die now. Shame could be the bridge to fall off of.

A strange hole manifested in Priyesh's heart, consuming him from the inside. The only thing he felt after a certain point was numbness, and everything went to black. No light. Just an essence of life... a vessel.

"Another Day in Fuckin' Paradise!" Priyesh heard Mary's voice, coming from a distance.

"Where am I?" he wondered.

A chair backed his spine. A table supported his elbow. A foreign grip held Priyesh's forearm firmly, suffocating the veins... it was turning pale.

"What's this?" Priyesh questioned. "But there's no pain, only an earthy odor of unfulfilled desires, of rotten dreams, of wasted potential.

A hand on the table—only a hand, nothing more, nothing less. Did this hand ever touch a loved one? Did it ever hold a glass of water? Was it able to conquer the battles its owner waged against the world and their own self?

The hand that turns everything it touches to gold—the hand of an artist, the greatest creator known to mankind—covered in bruises, brown with burned hair, stab wounds all over—was it even human? A hand that let go: The Hand of God.

***

"Another day in paradise!" Mary said, opening the curtains of the room, letting sunlight enter the room.

There were no other guests in the dorm except Mary and Priyesh.

"You are really the most eccentric motherfucker I know—randomly sitting on a chair with your arm on the table. You think too much, man!" Mary said.

Priyesh let out loud grunts, pushing his body away from the chair. His eyes were barely open, and his face was swollen.

"You look like you could use some sleep," said Mary.

"That is all I have been doing," Priyesh added.

"Then freshen up, and I'll take you to this beautiful Portuguese house I saw. It seems abandoned, and I thought that maybe you could translate if someone was inside the property. We could see some old furniture, man!" an excited

Mary said. "Also, this is my last day here, but I promise you, we will go to another beach soon!"

"What? You're leaving?" Priyesh questioned.

"Oh, I'm not leaving. I had booked another hostel that was closer to the beach because I wanted to work near the sea. This hostel is too far from the beach," Mary explained.

Priyesh remained silent.

"Also, I want coco!" Mary said.

"Coco?" Priyesh questioned.

"Coconuts," Mary replied. "They're my favorites. I found a vendor just a few minutes from the Portuguese house. We'll go there!"

"Sure!" Priyesh said.

The duo was out on the streets, walking towards an old Portuguese house that seemed possibly abandoned. Priyesh and Mary arrived at the property, guarded by a huge iron gate that was broken by a tree falling on it.

A small gap presented an entry, and Mary ran straight inside, asking her partner-in-crime to follow.

As soon as the two went inside, a number of dogs started barking, as if questioning the unknown humans regarding their business on the premises of the Portuguese house.

An old lady emerged out of the blue, questioning the two strangers. Priyesh took the initiative.

"Can we have a look inside? Miss Mary here would like to have a peek at the old relics that you might've kept in the house," Priyesh questioned in Hindi.

"Well, you'd have to talk to my son. He owns the land. Let me take you to him. He's in the yard," the old lady replied.

"She's so sweet and quite fit for her age," Mary replied. "Look at her adorable saree! Here, take a look at this picture I have on my phone. This was me in Delhi a few years ago with the Indian ex-boyfriend, wearing a saree."

"You look…fantastic! Magical," Priyesh said while the two followed the old lady to the backyard.

The huge yard was filled with palm trees, and the old lady's son was cutting them down, possibly to build a concrete house or a villa.

The son greeted the foreigner and the Indian, asking them about their requests.

Standing over six and a half feet tall, dark-skinned, and wearing a sun hat, the man greeted the travelers.

"We wanted to see the inside of the house," Mary said. "It seems exquisite—I'd love to see if you have old furniture and the decades-old walls of the house from the inside."

"Oh, sorry! We don't have anything to show. We're breaking down everything and rebuilding the entire structure—it is all sealed. So, no entry!" The old lady's son said.

"No worries. Thank you for your time," Mary replied.

As Priyesh and Mary walked back towards the gate, she said, "I'm sure he's lying. Let's take a peek around the back."

The two went towards the left side of the wall of the house, hoping to get a peek inside from the windows. But the windows were all bolted shut, and curtains prevented them from getting a look inside.

"Damn! I can't see shit," Mary said.

Priyesh went further ahead and started hopping on the ground, jumping higher each time to get a peek through the only window without a curtain.

The house was totally dark, and the air inside seemed heavy and secretive.

The walls screamed from the lack of light, reminiscing about the times when hands caressed over their entirety and spines took support on the walls.

"Miss Mary, come here. Have a look. You can see that there are cupboards and chairs inside that seem too old. The son lied to us!" Priyesh said.

"Well, what can we do? Let's go have coco, my work will soon begin," Mary said.

The duo walked all the way to the coconut vendor and back to the hostel. Around the reception area, Priyesh was greeted by Kunal, who said, "It's time for Redi Beach!"

"Yes! Let's go," Priyesh replied. "But first, let me have a smoke."

Priyesh ignited his cancer stick as one of the guests interrupted the conversation.

"Hi, I'm Aman," the stranger said, addressing Mary.

"I'm Marilyn; pleasure to meet you," said Mary while Priyesh stood aside, smoking his cigarette with Kunal.

"I don't know why people smoke or drink. I hate such habits, and I've never been friends with such people," Aman said.

It was clear what this stranger's intentions were.

"Don't judge! Although I don't smoke and drink occasionally, I can understand why people do it. You don't know what someone is going through, and from your remarks, it is clear that you're not interested in knowing. Every person has a reason to do what they do. Man, you have much work to do to be considered a decent human, much less a traveler," Mary said.

Aman knew he was meddling in a conversation where he wasn't needed and left, saying, "A few friends and I are going to the beach, and you're welcome to join!"

"Oh no, but thanks!" Mary replied.

She went on ahead to the dorm, asking Priyesh to wait for a bit, and a while later, she came back with her huge suitcase, adding, "This is goodbye. Give me your social media and share all the pictures with me. I'll keep you updated with my location, and we'll meet soon!"

"Sure! Take my number, send me a 'Hi,' and I'll send you the pictures. You promised that we'd go to the beach again, and I know you keep your promises and are not a traitor," said Priyesh.

"Don't you worry," Mary replied, giving Priyesh a tight hug and leaving for the other hostel she had booked.

For a few minutes, Priyesh stood still, watching Mary leave. It was one of those moments that you knew would happen but didn't know would happen so fast, and in the blink of an eye, the moment had passed as well. Kunal left the scene, went off to pack his bags, and got ready for the beach.

After releasing a deep sigh, Priyesh went towards the cafe.

A part of Priyesh was relieved that he would now be able to focus on his plans, while another part was just sad that Mary was leaving.

After she left in her tuk-tuk, Priyesh sat down on the same table where he had sketched half a face.

He continued his artwork, sketching ears after the nose was complete. The face that earlier seemed empty was gradually taking shape, seemed fuller, and resembled the person it was inspired by.

VI
Wasted Potential

"On some days, I wonder if you felt something, or was your heart too heavy with your own bullshit. We don't get that many chances at good people—they're rare. What you do—fucking up every time you meet someone good—that will land you nowhere: not good dead and useless alive," Anvi said during an argument she had with Priyesh not long ago.

The duo was seated on a two-wheeler, just like the painter and Kunal are—as of now—driving to Redi Beach from the hostel. Kunal took a special day off. He only got 2 a month, i.e., paid leaves.

"So, what do you want me to say?" Priyesh asked, frustratingly, speeding up the vehicle.

"I want you to show me that you have the balls to handle what you've been given instead of drowning over what you don't," said Anvi. "After all, there's no actual cause for your melancholy and suicidal behavior. You are romanticizing being sad, always under the spotlight—an attention-seeking, spineless soul."

Priyesh remained quiet but sped up the vehicle.

"I don't care if we die. You needed to face the truth," said Anvi.

The painter was silent, anger clouding the mind, thoughts, and morals.

The road to Redi passes through crowded places to secluded terrains, green all around with numbered tourists throughout the year. Forts, temples, and churches—a massive bridge through which you can see a massive chunk of the coastline.

"Hey, man! Why are you driving so fast?" Kunal asked.

"Huh? Is that so?" Priyesh wondered while looking at the meter. "Sometimes, I want to drive at fast speeds, maybe see if I have the balls to just leave the handle."

"Are you fucked in the head?" Kunal said.

"No, but still..." Priyesh said while being interrupted by Kunal.

"Check this bridge out! The beauty, my God," said Kunal while taking out his phone. "Don't you feel like you're leaving the land, leaning towards the sky—like everything'll be fine?"

"Are you fucking high?" Priyesh questioned. "Whatever, you're right, my bad."

Kunal was busy capturing the moments he did not want to miss.

The two continued to drive for around half an hour more, ending up on narrow, unpaved roads—wondering if they had come the wrong way.

After driving a few more minutes, watching snakes cross the road and frogs leaping in all their glory, the duo could see the coastline.

The duo hopped off their vehicle, bought a bottle of water, and went straight to the beach. The sundown was close.

"Let's just see the sun set and maybe chill for a while and have something to eat," said Priyesh.

"Oh yeah? Won't you like to go into the water?" asked Kunal, visibly disappointed.

"Ahh, no. I don't like getting wet," said Priyesh.

"Good that you don't have a pussy," said Kunal.

Priyesh laughed the insult off.

"Okay. Sorry! Cool, we won't go into the water," said Kunal.

"What's next then?" asked Priyesh.

"Let's sit, talk, and have some tea," Kunal added.

***

Close to the beach, the water was muddy and brownish, but not far from the land, the body of water turned blue. A little boy wearing shorts and with long hair was racing his younger sister.

"Definitely no one here is an Indian," said Priyesh.

"Apart from the color, what compels you to say this?" asked Kunal.

"You see that couple—naked, bathing in the sun. The two were looking like little soldiers who had lost their way during battle and decided to settle near the sea and spend their lives watching the sun set. This—you don't find this here. No one ever feels safe enough. Or better, no one feels enough," said Priyesh.

Kunal leaned closer to Priyesh, who reciprocated a similar move.

"Stop looking at people, or they'll call you a freak," whispered Kunal, bursting into laughter.

Between the island and the beach, the water changed colors frequently. Sometimes, it was light blue; other times, it was dark blue.

"The dark blue spots mean that the water at that place is quite deep," said Kunal.

"Is that so? Well, I don't know how to swim, and I am definitely never going inside," replied Priyesh.

The little boy ran across Priyesh and Kunal as the elder changed territories—sometimes in the water, other times on the sand.

"Look at him—I wish my parents raised me this close to nature. Heck, they didn't even push me to learn to swim. I guess it wasn't their fault. We were quite poor. Did what we could," Priyesh said.

"I was born into a rich family, but following the pandemic, everything went to shit. I finished my engineering, and somehow, due to a series of fucked-up events, I ended up in Goa. I was in Udaipur earlier and have some pretty good memories of that place," Kunal said.

"The pandemic fucked many. For my family, it was the cherry on top of the shit sandwich. Ah God! I wish I could tell whoever the fuck is writing my life that I am not a fly, cupping my hands every time I see rotting human waste," a visibly frustrated Priyesh blurted.

"You know. There was a friend of mine. He had this habit of constantly talking about shit. He would ask random people that he never met about the kind of shit they shat during their morning routine. Surprisingly, only a few went in the morning. Most people found peace during late evenings. I think these are what you'd call shy poopers," said Kunal.

"Cool," said Priyesh. "I am a shy pooper."

"Yeah, same," added Kunal.

"So, what happened to this dude?" Priyesh asked.

"Which dude," said Kunal, taking a sip of his tea.

"The shit one," emphasized Priyesh.

"Oh! He is a normal person, living a normal life somewhere close to his home. I heard he lost all his hair, became a drug addict, and is often reaching out to women from our circle for nudes and hookups. Even asked a couple for their sex tapes. They sold him two tapes!" Kunal revealed.

"Talk about scandalous information," Priyesh said. "But I meant to ask if he still talks about shit as much as he used to."

"Life straightened him out. He made a lot of conversations awkward with his 'shit talk' and poor habits. I never really understood why he was so bent on talking about shit all the motherfucking time," said Kunal.

"Forget him," said the painter. "So, you were saying something about Udaipur?"

"Oh fuck! Udaipur—the city that leaves a bittersweet taste in my mouth, like closing an eye that you have had opened for a while," said Kunal.

"What kind of description is that?" asked Priyesh.

"Yeah, it's a long story," said Kunal.

"I figured, but I wasn't asking about the length. I was asking about this bittersweet thing you were talking about," said Priyesh.

"Why the fuck do you explain everything so much? Chill out, dude," said Kunal.

"We have until sunset—about an hour or so," Priyesh replied.

"Cool. We have ample time," said Kunal.

"Go ahead." Priyesh gave a thumbs up.

"First, two of my questions—first, why didn't we have a foosball match today?" Kunal asked.

"I am so sorry. It was a weird morning," said Priyesh.

"Ok, cool. Next—people say let go; if it's meant for you, it will come back. The question is, I let go; she did not come back, but our love was real. Does that mean hers was fake, 'cause mine wasn't?" Kunal asked.

"See, I have loved some, and I let them go. They never came back. Does that mean that my love wasn't true? I don't know. If something is meant for you, it will happen. Maybe she wasn't meant for me, and the same applies to your case. But it all doesn't matter, trust me. At the end of the day, nothing matters; we're all like those stones sunk at the bottom of the sea—worthless until someone finds us, and we're unique and worth keeping in their eyes," Priyesh replied.

"That's the sad painter I was looking for!" exclaimed Kunal.

"You were telling me your story." Priyesh said in a softer, yet serious tone.

"A year ago, I fell for this woman at a hostel in Udaipur I was working for. She was the most beautiful person I had ever seen. Her eyes are similar to that muddy water near the beach. We spent some of the most beautiful moments together—traveling and spending a lot of nights planning our future, children, and everything. I even opened my own hostel when I was with her. You can call her my lucky charm," narrated Kunal.

"This all seems fine. Where is the shitty part?" Priyesh smirked.

"One fine day, she asked for my hand in marriage, and I wasn't ready because I had to build my own hostel business and be worth something," said Kunal, attempting to subdue the heaviness and rumble in his throat. "The partner with whom I opened the hostel was involved in some shady business, and authorities closed our property. She left me because she was looking for something more serious."

The two sat in silence for a while. Birds played with the fish in the sea—a game of life and death. The sun hugged everything for the last time, promising to visit again the next day, while the moon already awaited its time to shine.

***

A group of three was playing with a Frisbee—a yellow-colored disc with patches of paint coated on the inside.

A lady—beautiful, glorious, and at peace—played with sand while the two guys hopped around from one place to another.

"I think that guy with the heavy beard is pretty drunk. The hot one, who possibly came with the other guy—the hunk who looks like he just came from a posting in Kashmir," said Priyesh.

"Now that you say it out loud, this guy was definitely giving me Army vibes," said Kunal.

"Vibes? Really," said Priyesh.

"I tried. You're younger than me, don't forget," said Kunal.

"Cool. Cool," said Priyesh.

"I am going to pee," Kunal added, while getting up from his chair and leaving to find a spot to empty his bladder.

The drunk, bearded guy was soon getting out of control. He was soon obsessed with a dog that had found a new friend in him. With one leg forward, the dog would jump in the same direction—a game created without the exchange of any kind of words.

A lady entered with her dog on the beach.

"Dog, on this beach? Is this lady alright?" wondered Priyesh. "This is such a secluded and random spot for fancy people."

The dog, upon entering the beach, immediately attacked the drunk guy's dog. It was a full-blown rivalry the moment the two dogs tried to sink their teeth inside each other.

The fight was extremely cruel, one dog often overpowering the other. The drunk guy was not able to control the urge to help his dog and immediately picked up a rock to hit the other dog. A big-ass rock!

Then the other people with the drunk guy entered and calmed the situation.

"Ahh shit! A potential fight missed," mourned Priyesh as his eyes met with the drunk guy's.

Five minutes later, he came to the place where Priyesh was seated. Kunal was yet to arrive on the scene, and all Priyesh wished for was his friend's timely arrival.

"I am not good with drunk people," Priyesh reminded himself—possibly recalling past interactions.

"Hey man! I think you… you saw all the shit from moments ago. That fucker's dog scratched my beloved Simba. Blood everywhere. That is not justice. Do you know? A girl I love hasn't called me in weeks. Feel sad, hurt, dejec…ted. I can't let go of her. Every time I see her, I want to be with her, to be close to her breasts, to feel her heart, her warmth, her comfort," said the drunk man.

"No hesitation, huh? Guess you truly are heartbroken," said Priyesh. "Well, I am in the same boat as you, except I've found a solution."

"What solution?" asked the bearded guy.

"Death," said Priyesh with enough confidence to shake the world.

"Fuck off," said the guy.

"What? I am pretty serious about it. I have a date planned and all," said Priyesh.

"Ah yes? What is the date?" asked the drunk man.

"29th Feb," replied Priyesh.

"There is no 29th Feb. Fuck off, you fool," said the man while laughing out loud. "Also, if you die, what's the point?"

"I see, you don't have courage or sense," concluded Priyesh.

"Do you know how drunk I am? A lot! I have been smoking weed for the past two hours. Yet, I am sober enough to say that I will not die. I will come out of this a better person. But I really want to know, why did she leave me hanging? She fed her love and then beheaded me without remorse. What did I do to deserve such treatment?" wondered the drunk.

"Nothing. People are shitty. Everyone is mean and out to get you. They will find ways to strip you of your authenticity. I mean, I just wanted someone to have sex with and share my deepest regrets," Priyesh said while being cut off by the drunk guy.

"We're talking about me," the guy said.

"Ah, sorry," said Priyesh. "But you can fuck off because I have shit to do and not talk to a random dude like you. I have selected days. I want to die in peace."

A confused and clumsy drunk man left the scene while Kunal returned.

"Who was that?" asked Kunal.

"The drunk," replied Priyesh.

"Well, fuck him. You know, it dawned on me that the woman I told you about—our relationship was wasted potential. It could've been something great, but eventually, it was just crushed, like a dream," said Kunal.

"The drunk guy and now you. C'mon, man, the sun has set. Let us leave. Women are not worth it—love is not worth it, and lately, I've seen enough to say—even life is not worth it," said Priyesh.

Kunal remained silent, lost in a life he had left behind a long time ago.

The duo reached their two-wheeler. Priyesh turned one last time to see the drunk guy—his head under the water, arms struggling to find the surface. The concerned friends were panicking, possibly looking for a swimmer.

"They'll save him," thought Priyesh, quickly starting the two-wheeler.

If it wasn't meant for me, why was it mine?
If I can't have it back, that's fine.

Was it a lie or a hope that I believed in?
Was my need—
The need to be loved—a sin?

No reverse, there is no reset—
I cannot erase that we met.

I wear my heart on my sleeve,
I smile despite all my grief.
If she is meant to be in my life,
She will be my wife.

If not:
Then I say no to such a life.
Claim me, O' water,
Dissolve me; leave no matter.

My love lost its meaning in her eyes,
The desires of the heart:
My breath paid the price.

VII
Drunk?

"Another day in fucking paradise!" Mary exclaimed. "Wakey wakey!"

"But you left?" Priyesh wondered, trying to capture Mary's presence inside of his eyes.

"I did. Yet, here I am. I often wonder, though," she said.

"What? What do you wonder, Miss Mary?" Priyesh said, vision still blurry, throwing his arms all over the place to capture the vessel that contained the sweet voice.

A minute passed by, all efforts in vain.

"Where are you, Mary?" Priyesh asked.

"So close to you," whispered Mary in the painter's ears.

"Did you come back for me?" Priyesh said, once again attempting to capture the mermaid.

"I can't see you. Everything is a blur. There is no concrete imagery I can see of you—only a voice, but how do I hold you, picture you, paint you?" asked Priyesh.

Priyesh got up from the bed, eyes still blurry. He kept rubbing his eyes, waving his arms around to balance and navigate the room.

Inside the washroom, Priyesh faced the mirror—splashing water all over his face.

"You're back, I see," Anvi said.

"Anvi?" said Priyesh.

"What brings you back every damn time? My voice? My body? Or your desires?" Anvi interrogated.

"You left. You don't care. I don't care," blurted Priyesh, rubbing soap across his face.

"You can't see, can you? Still the same blind idiot. Here, take my hand," said Anvi.

Priyesh felt a hand close to his chest—his vision still blurry.

The closer the hand came, the safer Priyesh felt in his temporary blindness.

"I never felt this safe with you around. 'Will she break the bulb today or my face?' that was all I could think of back then," Priyesh said.

He grabbed the hand coming towards himself in a hurry.

"I am so sorry. I didn't mean it. It was nice to be with you. I know I am not a competent person, but can't we stay together? At least for now? Until my vision returns?" Priyesh asked.

Silence was the only answer he got.

"Anvi? Mary?" Priyesh called out their respective names multiple times, holding a foreign hand.

Priyesh pulled the hand closer to his chest, and it grabbed the painter's neck, suffocating him. No words. No whispers. No resistance. The grip grew stronger.

The painter's vision got slightly clearer as the grip grew stronger. The face turned red. Priyesh was stuck with a death he didn't want to see.

A bruised hand manifested in front of Priyesh, who tried getting away but couldn't. It seemed familiar, yet the intentions were darker. This time the hand had bigger and filthier nails and an intense odor. A piece of blue cloth was stuck to it.

The pain soon turned the painter's body cold. Priyesh lost consciousness, tears falling from his eyes. The hand let Priyesh's neck go as he failed to maintain balance.

His head felt extremely numb, his body light—contact with the hard floor was inevitable.

BAM!—like they say in the comics—a thud was heard: Priyesh rolling on the floor.

"Ouch," he screamed.

"What happened, sir?" said a man in red.

"Who are you?" asked the painter.

"I'm Satvik. Who are you my friend, falling from the bed like a six-year-old does after realizing that he wasn't just peeing in a dream?" he said.

"You're drinking already? In the morning?" Priyesh asked.

"I have been drinking since I stepped foot here. Also, it is already evening. Brother, what you see in my hand—this rotten hand holds a beer bottle. You know, this is my 35th beer pint since last night. I fucking love it here," said the stranger.

"Well, call me Priyesh. I'm a painter," he replied.

***

"One more, please!" Satvik said while almost falling from his chair in the cafe. His eyes had almost shut, and he reeked of alcohol.

"Oh, come on! I think it has been enough," said Priyesh.

"It's crazy, man!" Satvik said while asking for another bottle.

He already had an almost-full bottle in his hand. Satvik pulled it closer—a few drops of beer escaped from the container and fell.

"The beer feels pity for you. It won't go in your stomach, it seems," said Kunal, who stood close by.

"Let's get something to eat," said Satvik, using his other hand to indicate his hunger.

"Get him another one," Kunal told Ren, the bartender.

"Sure?" Ren whispered.

"It's his tab. Why should we care?" Kunal replied.

"Coming right up," Ren told Satvik.

"Bring one for these two as well. On me!" Satvik shouted, startling those around him.

"What a mess!" exclaimed Kunal.

"Do you guys know why I'm drinking so much today?" Satvik asked.

"Well, why?" Priyesh replied.

"It is the one-year anniversary of me meeting my father for the first time in my life," said Satvik.

"What?" Kunal asked.

"Well, my mother's sister raised me since I was young. According to her, both my mother and father had died. As I grew up, on my eighteenth birthday, I was told that my father—who had supposedly passed away—was alive," Satvik recalled.

"What's your age right now?" asked Priyesh.

"I forget. Well, back to the story. Two years later, I am sitting in a cafe with my girlfriend and now ex-girlfriend when a hand dressed in blue lands on my right shoulder from behind. I look at this man, and I know he is my father. I swear, I look exactly like him," said Satvik.

"Then?" asked Kunal and Priyesh simultaneously.

"He asked me how I was and if I needed anything. I didn't know what to make of it. I was astounded. I wanted to hug him, but I was pissed off that he never tried to approach me until I was twenty," said Satvik.

"So, then what happened?" Priyesh asked.

"I told my aunt about this encounter, and she advised me to never meet him again. I was persistent and questioned why. She revealed that my father killed my mother, adding that I was sent far away so he won't reach me," Satvik said.

"Fuck, man!" exclaimed Kunal, widening his eyes.

"My girlfriend started distancing herself from me soon after because maybe my issues were too huge to handle, and we gradually broke up," said Satvik as his eyes started to tear.

"Shit," said Priyesh while looking at Kunal's face, wondering if their ex-girlfriends were much better at caring for them.

Satvik asked for another beer, but Kunal intervened, eventually taking him towards his dorm room.

"Damn," a stunned Priyesh said.

Ren returned and asked, "What happened? Where did Kunal and the drunk go? I got the beer."

"It's a long story, mate. You need to hear it from Kunal. If he asks for me, tell him I'm in my room," said Priyesh, exiting the cafe.

***

"Shit! How could I have made this mistake? I'm fucked. I need to deactivate my social media handle immediately. Fuck. Fuck. Fuck!" a girl in Priyesh's room said.

The painter was curious but ignored the chaos and decided to check his phone.

"Hey Priyesh! This is my new hostel. Look at that. Everything is adorable and raw. I'm in love with this. There are little lamps, and the fun fact is that it is 1 minute from the beach. It would've been enjoyable to have you over here. I actually made a new friend as well. Obviously, it's not like you'll be the only one that I meet during this entire trip, haha! Let's meet up soon, kisses," Mary text read, accompanied with 32 images.

A smile took hold of Priyesh's face.

"That's cool. I can't change hostels so frequently. I've already paid for the days I'm here, and thereafter, I don't really know what will happen. So, it'll be cool to see you again. Hit me up, and we'll go to the clubs you mentioned," Priyesh replied.

"Hey man!" The girl in Priyesh's dorm said.

"Fuck! You just scared me," Priyesh said.

"They moved me here after an idiot crept out this morning," said the girl.

"What happened?" Priyesh asked.

"So, there was this guy... Wait a minute. Do you smoke? We can continue the story on the balcony, over a smoke," the girl added.

"Sure! I'm Priyesh," he said.

"I'm Anamika," the girl said while moving towards the balcony door in a hurry, claiming a chair.

"I fucked up big today. I posted a picture of my boyfriend and me on my social media, and my cousins and aunts have seen the picture. I don't know what to do," Anamika said.

"Well, you can tell them that he's a friend or some influencer you're a fan of," Priyesh suggested.

"Not a bad idea, dude," Anamika replied. "Well, I have to go!"

"What? You're leaving already?" asked Priyesh.

"Yeah. I mean, no! My boyfriend's coming to get me. I have to get ready, and then I will leave," said the girl.

Priyesh left the dorm, once again marching towards the cafe. He saw Kunal, seated alone adjacent to the table where the painter was drawing a sketch—a work in progress.

"So, what happened to Satvik?" asked Priyesh, pulling out a chair and a pencil.

"Well, he vomited in the dorm. The girls came and complained. He also behaved inappropriately with some of the women in the hostel. Sid immediately requested that he leave the premises. So he did," Kunal said.

Priyesh was listening, but his mind was lost on the next steps for his sketch.

"You won't have to pay for the table even if you take it with you in the dark of the night," Kunal said.

"What do you mean?" Priyesh asked.

"This hostel will be closing soon, mate!" Kunal said.

"When?" Priyesh interrogated.

"On the day you're checking out," Kunal added.

"What!" Priyesh exclaimed.

"Yeah. Well, I'm exhausted and a little drunk because of Satvik. I'll sleep and see you soon," said Kunal.

Priyesh sat alone in the cafe, attempting to carve the sketch his heart wanted to.

Minutes later, Anamika came down the stairs in a beautiful reddish-pink dress that ended near the knees. She applied a little makeup to her cheeks and turned them red. Her eyes wore a shade of pink, while her red sandals made it difficult for her to walk.

Priyesh couldn't take his eyes off her—seemingly perfect in that moment. "Wow," he said, beginning with his sketch.

"Damn, girl! You're so fucking hot," Priyesh said.

"I know!" said Anamika while blushing. "A picture with me—that is what you get for saving my ass today. Your idea worked!"

"I could just look at you for a while—woman, you're a work of art!" Priyesh said.

"Thanks, but enough! I'm leaving. Hope to see you someday," said Anamika.

Once again, Priyesh, alone, started to work on his artwork on the table, gradually piecing together a face that he failed to recognize.

"If there was no emotion, would there be art? The fading away of labyrinthine sentiments associated with self-pity borne from the sadness of depleted desires—deep down, everyone wants to die," whispered a voice in Priyesh's ears—a hand on his right shoulder—a hand with extremely filthy nails.

The painting started to take shape,
One eye, a nose, and a thin face—
Out of imagination, the materials he would scrape.
Was this the final project: his fate?

A face that wouldn't even last long.
What is the point? What is he even doing anymore?
Everyone is fucked up: life doesn't taste like before.

Whether to take the red pill or the blue,
A question he has to answer, true—
A question he must answer within:
Before answering me and you.

VIII

Hooked Up

"Can you help me, please?" a girl in a white shirt and black pants asked.

"Sure!" Kunal said.

"I need a different room ASAP. There was this guy in the six-bed dorm, a creepy dude. He told me I was pretty... what the fuck? Well, I want a private room or possibly an upgrade," the girl said.

"Well, let me have a look," Kunal said.

Priyesh had been sitting in the same chair since last night, obsessed with the sketch he was trying to put together.

"Well, I'm upgrading you to the 4-bed dorm, free of charge. You can have a look. Priyesh is staying there. He's a painter, and he's family," said Kunal.

"I'll have a look," the girl said, leaving the premises.

Moments later, she came back, anxious. She was on a call, discussing next moves.

Flustered, she came towards Kunal. "I need a private room! I can't stay in the dorm. The painter guy is a man. Might be a good person, but I don't take chances," the girl said.

"Ma'am, you need to understand, the private rooms are all booked. The 4-bed dorm is all we have," Kunal said.

"In that case, I don't have a choice, do I? Give me the 4-bed dorm," the girl said, losing her argument.

The afternoon heat troubled Priyesh, and so he decided to take a cold shower, leaving for his room as well.

***

"Hi, I'm Kaira. There was this guy in the six-bed dorm where I was staying, and this guy popped up out of nowhere, calling me pretty in a creepy way. I mean, girls are sharp as tacks—we know what men think once they have a look at us. Not everyone is happy with being hit on, and I have a boyfriend as well," the girl said.

"Cool," said Priyesh, coming out of the shower

You're not the only one sad,
Nor the only one who's faced the bad—
Decaying as time passes, piling up losses,
You put pressure on the wounds.
Drowning them beneath a surface that glosses.

The emptiness that your heart has housed,
It takes a while to get used to it and not get aroused.

Again and again, you try to find,
Again and again, you use your mind.
But you're looking to find—
A reason to live more, a reason to grind.

Look no further, 'cause one fine day,
You'll leave it all behind and lie silent and true—
With much to say, but won't be able to.

***

"Let's go to this cafe," said Kaira.

"What?" asked the painter.

"Sure, why not?" the girl said. "I'll tell you my story—not like we are seeing each other again."

Around 4 PM, the duo left the hostel and decided to visit a cafe, traversing narrow lanes of the beautiful Parra village, where the trees belittle you from both sides of the road.

Kaira and Priyesh went inside a cafe, seated close to the reception and the display cases for pastries, cakes, donuts, and cookies. There were Europeans, Americans, Israelis, and a handful of Indians sitting, working, smoking, and chatting in the cafe.

"Hello, sir," said the manager at the reception. "Here's our menu. You can connect to the WiFi as well. The password is in front of you. Let us know what you'd like to have."

"Wow. Fancy! I would like to have an eclair," Priyesh said.

"Would you like a mango shake or cold coffee for drinks, and maybe a salad for food?" the manager proposed.

"Nah. No food. Get me an eclair and an Americano," said Priyesh.

"Sure," said the manager, passing the order to the cook.

"How long have you been in Goa?" Priyesh questioned the manager.

"I've been here for a few years. I was actually born here. My parents died in a crash when I was young, so I was sent to Delhi for studies," said the manager.

"Well, then, you must have a lot of parental land here. I'm sure you're the cafe owner as well," Priyesh concluded.

"No," said Fernandez with a forced laugh. "I was just 8 when my parents died, and my relatives sent me to my aunt's in Delhi. When I grew up and came back, it turned out that my parental property was already sold to a local hotshot by some relative."

"Shit! I'm so sorry!" Priyesh said.

"My entire childhood, I dreamt of opening a cafe in Goa, leaving a legacy. I guess I was wrong. You know, life never stops teaching you, but after a point, you just don't want to learn. I'm 35, working at a cafe, earning minimum wage when I could've been like every other rich cafe owner in Goa," said the manager.

Silence prevailed.

"I'll have this and this," interrupted Kaira, pointing out what she wanted to have.

"What do you paint about?" Kaira asked as the manager left.

"Right now, I am working on my last painting. Don't know much about it," said Priyesh.

"You did the sketch on the table, right? In the cafe? You've got insane skills," praised Kaira.

"Thank you!" Priyesh smiled.

"Is it so easy for me to get infatuated?" Priyesh wondered.

"Hey! So, would you like to tell a stranger what's troubling you?" Priyesh asked after a few minutes of silence.

"Um, I guess there is no harm in disclosing a secret to a stranger. We're obviously not meeting after Goa," said Kaira.

"That's a given," said Priyesh, who was slightly let down by this statement. "But don't say it again and again."

"Well, I am a victim of sexual abuse, and it was someone quite close to me who violated me from when I was a child until the day I went to college. One day, I resisted, and it finally stopped. That's just it," Kaira said.

"What? I have so many questions. Firstly, who was it? A cousin? A relative? Did you ever tell your parents about it?" Priyesh asked.

Kaira remained quiet, refraining from uttering a single word.

"Don't tell me. Was it someone close? Your cousin? Brother? Fuck no! Was it your father?" Priyesh threw all the worst guesses out in the open.

"My father," said Kaira, smiling. "You know, there was a toxic ex-boyfriend of mine as well. That son of a bitch used to restrict my movements and sometimes hit me. We were together for years. He knew about my father."

Priyesh had no words to say. "Fuck" was the only thing that came out of his mouth.

"Well, I've found a good man who treats me well. I don't know how long this will last, but he is cool. Honestly, I'm more into traveling nowadays. Whenever I get the time, I just come here and go to the mountains—anywhere," she added.

"So, the only question I think I should ask, without scraping old wounds, is, how can your father still face you?" Priyesh asked.

"He left my mother for a while when we were young. Now that I've gotten over that shit and my mother and little brother are finally happy, I don't want to ruin the good we have. Nobody knows. I keep my mouth shut, and everything is fine. My father did what he did. I don't care about it anymore," Kaira said.

The duo silently finished their meals, reaching the hostel without talking much.

***

The sun had already set. Priyesh and Kaira were having dinner together.

"I am leaving tomorrow," she said.

"Already?" Priyesh asked.

"Yeah, well, my boyfriend is with his best friend right now, and I don't trust her around him," Kaira said.

"I feel you," Priyesh said.

"Well, cheers," said Kaira, drinking up the alcohol she had ordered a while ago.

Hours passed as the two chatted. A game was held at the hostel's cafe too. Everyone had to sing something or say something—it was an open mic.

The duo sang a shitty song in their drunken voices. It was a mess. Kunal and Sid managed to get the duo the room they were allotted.

"Damn!" said Priyesh. "I think we pissed a lot of people off today."

"Who cares?" said Kaira, holding Priyesh's arm while removing her sandals as she entered the room.

"Oh, I wish my boyfriend were here. We would've made such sweet love," wished Kaira.

While entering the room, Kaira clenched the painter's hand too tightly, and as he lost balance, he fell to Kaira's level.

"It has been a while since I had an orgasm," said Kaira.

"What?" Priyesh asked. "That's a bummer."

"Someone should fix that," said Kaira.

"Really?" asked Priyesh, pressing his hand gently over her face.

"Yep," said Kaira.

Priyesh leaned in for a kiss. Kaira reciprocated. The soft touches of the lips gradually turned wilder as the two embraced their lust.

The painter immediately pushed Kaira on his bed.

"Ouch," he said while hitting the bed bunked above his own bed.

"Haha," Kaira started to laugh.

"Fuck," said Priyesh, immediately grabbing Kaira's left butt cheek and squeezing it. The girl's brown pants started turning moist with Kaira whispering what she felt.

The duo lay beside each other, Kaira's head on Priyesh's left arm, as if a soft stem were supported by a stick—taking his right hand inside her brassiere.

Priyesh took deep breaths, caressing the depth of femininity with his hard dick. The moisture was now visible clearly. The painter grabbed the right butt cheek, touching the vagina from over the pants using his crotch.

Kaira took deep breaths as Priyesh got further aroused. He grabbed the girl's neck from the sides, pulling her body towards his.

The duo stared at each other, and then Priyesh freed the nipples from their cage, using his tongue to pleasure Kaira, who was sober enough to feel what she wanted—free.

Priyesh got on top of Kaira, who wasn't ready.

"Hey," she said. Priyesh did not listen, losing himself.

Kaira held Priyesh's face, leaning in for a kiss. He returned the kiss but with more aggression, slapping the girl after the kiss ended.

"Oh fuck!" Priyesh exclaimed, snapping out of his horny state. "I am so sorry. Fuck! Are you hurt?"

Kaira pushed Priyesh away, closed the lights, and went to sleep.

The next morning, Kaira was already gone by the time Priyesh woke up. No goodbye, no small talk, and no contact.

The painter dragged his body all the way to the cafe to work on his painting.

"Another day in fuckin' paradise," he said.

IX

Where the Land Meets the Sea

Five days in, Priyesh had yet to complete his artwork. By now, he had this notion that the sketch on the table would be his masterpiece. However, the longevity of the project concerned him.

"Hey!" Mary called out Priyesh from one of the shops in the market. "Come here."

Priyesh took his wallet—a shabby leather one, brown in color, gifted by Anvi a year ago on his birthday—taking some money out.

"Here, take this," he said, paying the shopkeeper and buying a silver bracelet for his German friend.

The two greeted each other. "Been a few days," Mary said.

"Yeah!" Priyesh said.

The two avoided gazes as an awkward silence prevailed. Priyesh failed to understand why Mary had not set up a meeting in the past few days if she liked him.

"So, where are you staying?" asked Priyesh.

"Just behind this market lane—there's a house. A beautiful kitchen close to the beach. Amazing views," said Mary.

"Cool," said Priyesh, following Mary around in the colorful market.

"Do you think I should buy these shirts?" Mary questioned, holding one next to her face.

"Yeah, sure. But they're for males," Priyesh said.

"I know, I'm not an idiot. The shirts are for the boyfriend I told you about," Mary said.

The painter's smile was cut in half, one falling on a bed of hopes, the other crashing at the bottom of the ocean of jealousy and despair.

"Hey! Can we click a picture with you?" A middle-aged man questioned the German, stopping the duo midway.

Not giving him a room to breathe, the man and his wife held the German by the shoulders, clicking pictures.

Mary was forced to share a smile. Many don't mean harm but are poisonous nonetheless. Many.

The lady took Mary for herself as the old man came closer to Priyesh.

"How did you meet her?" he inquired.

"We were together in a hostel," said Priyesh.

The man, confused, asked, "Such facilities in hostels?"

"Hey, let's go," said Mary. "It's weird. C'mon!"

"Yes, Miss Mary," said Priyesh.

"What was he saying?" asked Mary.

"Gibberish," said Priyesh. "If he tried something, I would've sent him straight to heaven."

"Where is this aggression coming from, man? First of all, never ever try to protect me. I can do everything on my own. I've been traveling for years. I know how to get around idiots," asserted Mary.

"Got it," said Priyesh.

"Promise me," stated Mary.

"Yeah, I promise," Priyesh agreed.

Mary wore an ocean-green top covered in pink flowers. Her dresses were always colorful.

"I've traveled to 34 countries in the past few years and visited all the places I wanted to see. I even saw where they shot the Pirates of the Caribbean movies. Just want to do another US trip soon," Mary shared. "You should go."

"Maybe," said Priyesh, smiling.

"You know, people in Germany are always dressed up like they have no life—there is no color. Everything is just bland. The winters there are the worst," Mary said.

"If you hate it there, why are you going back?" Priyesh asked.

"Back in my twenties, I used to party my ass off. Soon, I went broke. Now, I've realized that in order to keep traveling, I need to have a plan that would get me money, and money will get me freedom to do anything. It's not easy, but it can be done," Mary said.

"Well, on the positive side, you don't have that regret, right? That you failed to live your twenties the way you wanted to," Priyesh asked.

"Of course not! I had a lot of sex, was with a lot of amazing people, made cool friends, and saw everything I wanted to. I was in Greece and Spain, two of the most amazing trips of my life. Damn, you should definitely go there. It's amazing!" Mary said.

Priyesh once again smiled at the irony of the situation.

"Of all the times you chose to make me feel alive—it is the closest to my death," thought Priyesh.

The two stopped their walk around the market and sat in a small cafe. The structure was clearly temporary, standing very close to the beach—one rainfall or extreme wind away from losing its balance.

"You know, Miss Mary, I actually missed how you'd get up every morning and wake me up with 'another day in paradise.' I've met a few cool people, but damn, you've been irreplaceable," said Priyesh.

"Don't get too attached, you idiot. One fine day, either of us will leave Goa," said Mary.

"I wonder. When I'm 50, and you're, I don't know what, it'll be so amazing to look back and maybe have a conversation about the few days we spent in Goa," said Priyesh.

"Well, I don't care. Even if I am old, I will age with grace—you'll still find me fucking guys much younger than me!" Mary exclaimed.

"Miss Mary, I kind of like you," Priyesh blurted with the last drop of the sun's light drying up in the presence of the cold night breeze.

"I actually like you too. It was fun with you in the hostel and at Baga Beach," Mary said.

The painter was happy, and yet the German's intentions were alien to him.

"Will she?" Priyesh wondered. "Will she fuck me?"

***

"Where have you been? We had an awesome night here, man!" Bobo said.

"I was at a club with Mary," said Priyesh.

"Oh! The foreigner, right?" Bobo asked.

"Yep," said Priyesh.

"Cool, cool," Bobo stated.

"I made a new cocktail today from feni, the local drink. You should try it, man—chili, salt, lemon, and a few other things," Ren said.

"Sure!" Priyesh said.

Kunal returned from the washroom.

"Welcome back! We've been looking for you. There were a few arts college students from Jaipur who looked at the sketch you drew on the table and were mesmerized. They wanted to talk to you," said Kunal.

"Sure," Priyesh said.

"You know, I sometimes sketch too," said Nitin.

"Oh really? Show me," said Priyesh, taking Nitin to a corner of the cafe.

"I will," said Nitin, turning towards a wall.

"Why don't you draw more often? I never saw you doing something," said Priyesh.

"It is not easy to become an artist. You would know that. Plus, I have responsibilities. I wanted to be a sketch artist, and now look at me serving orders at a hostel. I never expected that my life would turn out like this. Now I'm due to be married; the girl wants me to reduce weight, and my mother wants her to quit her job. Everything is fucked," said Nitin.

Silence took over as a text dropped on Priyesh's device. It was from Anvi. The painter wondered if he should reply this time.

She came into your life unexpectedly,
You thank her wholeheartedly.
She hugged and healed your heart—
A distinct relation from the start.

You miss her; you long to kiss her,

She might not feel the same—
Her presence has made you insane.

You both are seas apart,
Yet you were never so alive in your heart.
You will leave, taking her memories with you,
A black rose, a miracle that happened to you.

You were lucky to have met a mermaid,
They're rare to come by, much rarer to see.
Maybe, one fine day, you will meet her at a place,
Where the land meets the sea.

***

"I will dedicate the world to you," the writer said.

"You're in a dream—delusional, wanting to live what you wrote," the girl replied.

"What makes you think this isn't a dream anyway?" the boy questioned.

"If this is a dream, I'd pray for it to be over," said the girl.

"Maybe I don't want to wake up; maybe this was always about wanting to sleep forever, in an endless slumber," he told his delusional self as the girl stormed out, leaving the writer with more questions than answers.

Years later, they met at a shop, where the sun meets the sea—accidentally.

"How come you're here?" the girl asked the boy.

"I don't know! Maybe this wasn't some dream, after all?" the boy said.

"You dummy. Still as stubborn as ever, I see," the girl added.

"I have written so much; it can't all be delusional, can it?" questioned the boy.

"Let's order something!" the girl suggested.

Their talks continued in a cafe on a land where you can see the sun and the sea as one.

No doubt many people live there. People with stories that refused to rot in the land of forgotten lovers—where the question 'what if' manifests in reality; where love wasn't elusive all the time.

X

Chidiya

"Four days," said Priyesh the next day he woke up, staring at the curtains.

"Curtains don't remove themselves, do they?" he wondered, tilting his head, closing his eyes, and silencing the noise for a bit. "Mary is leaving soon too!" Panic had set in. Time was limited. The sketch is incomplete.

The painter immediately ran towards the cafe. A couple had occupied the table where his artwork was engraved.

"Move over!" Priyesh came running as the couple immediately left the table, anxious and worried if something grave lay beneath it.

Priyesh began sketching, not giving a fuck about what he had just done.

He started giving final touches to the face he had spent days engraving on the table. The eyes were perfect—both irises of different shades. Leafy eyelashes and lips fuller on the left while being thinner on the right.

The inspiration behind the sketch came from various people, and among all the characters the painter tried to showcase, his own was missing.

I am incomplete; I am scared of the stare,
It's getting hard for me now;
Life is getting extra tough on me; it's not fair.

It feels like I've lasted long enough,
My mind, body, and soul —
Have all started giving up,
It all just feels so tough.

Can't see through me anymore;
I can't sleep, just yawn—
Can't bear my own thoughts;
All I can do is bleed from dusk until dawn.

Nothing feels real now;
Everything is meaningless—
It's crystal clear now.
A question arises in my mind:
'Are many people like me, or is it just me somehow?'

My soul has gone stale;
I'm done. I can't tell you my tale.

Maybe I want to go far away;
I'm tired—
Tired of waiting in this fuckin' paradise,
Another sun, another day.

***

Not long after, the swimming pool was quiet—the cleaning staff nowhere to be seen.

The kitchen was closed too, and all the windows were bolted shut. The silence made Priyesh uneasy.

A headache haunted the painter—the kind that feels like a nail penetrating your head, blood gushing out like soda from a bottle once you shake it.

"Fuck, man," said Priyesh out loud. "I feel like throwing up, but I don't really like throwing up."

He came out of the cafe, close to the pool, and saw a bird. It was huge and seemed scary. The animal spread its wings, trying to fly away, but whenever it did, its head would smash into the glass fence that enclosed the cafe.

For the bird, the glass was as beneficial as air; it couldn't understand why, despite numerous attempts, it was unable to get out.

Priyesh stood close to the bird for a couple of minutes, observing its attempts to try and push through. No one was around to help, and eventually, the painter intervened.

Of course, he was afraid that the large bird might scratch him. He tried to touch the bird, but it would enlarge its wings, warning Priyesh to maintain distance.

After all, how can a bird have faith in a man, and vice versa? Humans never stuck to a belief, and animals never tried to accept anything other than what they believed.

He decided to have a cigarette and think about what to do.

While smoking, he kept searching for a solution as the bird continued attempting to fly away but couldn't for some reason. His eyes wandered across the cafe and reception, not stumbling on anything useful.

After a few minutes of thorough searching, Priyesh saw a mic stand with an iron circular base. An idea clicked.

He picked up the mic stand and placed it right near the bird's feet. The bird continued moving around its wings haphazardly—warning the painter while also pushing its body higher.

Slowly, Priyesh started pulling the stand into the air, and the bird's feet landed on the circular base of the mic stand. The bird was impatient. As a result, the rescue operation took a few attempts.

After a productive fifteen minutes, the bird finally made a swift move towards the sky through a hole while Priyesh brought the mic stand's base to the level of the top of the glass fence.

The bird left a part of its black and brown feather as a gift. He took the feather, once again making his way towards the table to take a gander at his last artwork.

The moments you're thinking about,
Let them float away:
They don't exist anyway.

It was the past;
The time gone seems sweeter than berry,
And I know you want it to come back in a hurry.

Believe me, it was fine if they left.
Like a tall tower,
You shall stand silent and bereft—
After a storm drained you of joy,
Don't worry:
We all find our places;
It is all some random's ploy.

Let these waves take your sorrow far from you.
Alas, the waves can't soak me,
For I challenged the sea too.

***

"Hey Priyesh!" Kunal said. "Let's play our last foosball game today," Kunal said.

"Why last?" Priyesh asked.

"Because in two days, after you check out of the hostel," informed Kunal. "You're one of the last people to see this place. This foosball table is going to be sold today, along with some other stuff—the chairs and the tables. However, I've convinced them to leave the table with your sketch here. You'll have to pay around 1,000 INR, and that's it."

"Yeah, I'll pay," Priyesh said.

His heart suddenly started to beat faster. The headache was back. He was losing his calm composure. It was the time to face his decision now: death.

The two began to play foosball. Priyesh was preoccupied with unexplained feelings, and his head was being crucified.

With the mind in a state of bedlam, Priyesh couldn't figure out when or how to hit the ball.

Kunal scored the first goal and then another. "Focus," he told Priyesh.

Priyesh took a deep breath. After some back-and-forth movement, the game came to a halt when both scored nine goals each.

By now, five people, including three girls and two boys, possibly quite young, were watching the game with tremendous interest. As the ball approached Priyesh's rod, he pushed it too hard, and it broke into two pieces.

"What the fuck?" exclaimed Bobo at the reception. "This is total bullshit, man!"

Priyesh immediately fled the scene, suggesting that he had a call. Upon reaching his room, his phone vibrated. He saw a text from Anvi.

"Hey Priyesh. Long time, no text or call. How have you been holding up? I haven't heard from you in a while, and I was worried. Where are you? Call me. I need to..." the text read.

Priyesh did not bother to read the entire thing. The phone once again vibrated.

"This place will soon close. Miss Mary will soon leave. What will you do then? There is no one to have your back. What have you learned in all these days—anything? What is this dilemma? Just go ahead and do it," Anvi texted.

Priyesh sat down on one of the stairs as the group of five young adults passed him by while he was looking at the feather, gifted by the bird earlier.

Out of the five, one stayed—a girl in a bold red dress, dusky skin, innocent eyes, and hair black as a killer's heart—smiling, as if a madman surfing the waves of chaos.

"It is the middle of the afternoon, and in this heat, why are you sitting on stairs with a feather? My guess is that's a Bharadwaj, I mean a greater coucal. By the way, I'm Priya," the girl who stayed said.

"I did not get a word you said," Priyesh said.

"My name?" she asked, acting coy. "I'm Priya. The bird's name is Bharadwaj. My mother used to say it is very lucky to see, much less touch, this bird."

"Woah," said Priyesh.

"Apologies if I reek of alcohol. I need alcohol to talk to strangers now," Priya said, manifesting a laugh—nothing too fancy; she sounded just like a normal drunk girl. Yep.

"Well, all this trip, I've been trying to fit in. The five of us came from Jaipur. All we have done is visit cafes here. I wanted to see the nightlife and the beaches, but they are all wussies. Plus, many people among us like to hog the spotlight, if you know what I mean," added Priya.

"You've got some complaints," Priyesh replied.

"It is not just this. There are romantic complications, my college is going to shit—the final exams are here, and after graduation, I don't know what I will do. It is so fucked up," said Priya.

"Tell me about it. At the end of the day, I fail to feel the need to breathe," Priyesh confessed.

"What the hell, dude! You just went in a completely different direction," laughed Priya. "It isn't that bad. I am, in fact, we are much better than the majority of people sleeping in the streets."

"At least they have control," said Priyesh.

"They don't," said Priya. "Nobody has any control. We just try to do better each day. Despite knowing the better shit to do, we don't. Ungrateful, that's what we are."

"You were just complaining about your life!" exclaimed Priyesh.

"Yeah. But c'mon, dying because life is bad—not good. Here, take my hand," said Priya.

"Hand? I don't see it," an anxious Priyesh blurts, feeling sick in his stomach.

Looking down, he saw blood painting a hand red. The scars on the hand drank the gushing life from the stomach—luckily there was no pain, only fear.

The intensity and flow of blood was rising. Priyesh moved his head up in complete shock; his eyes froze while open. All he could do was watch as the outflow of blood fourfolded in just minutes.

The tongue doesn't work if it's terrified. The painter looked down again, pressuring his hand to move, but to no avail.

The hand refuses to give up, stuck deep inside Priyesh's stomach. Yet there was no anguish.

Soon, darkness emerged in the corner of his eyes, and the pain manifested. It was hell. All the pain, at once, waiting for the painter's last breath.

The eyes began closing for the first time in minutes. A hand that haunted the painter—scarred, poisonous, and suffocating due to the worsening smell with each encounter.

The second hand, a human's—it was Priya's—soon landed on the painter's cheek. A face came closer; a kiss followed. There was no hand lodged in the stomach. The pain was gone. The eyes were finally shut.

The foul odor was replaced with alcohol breath. Priyesh tasted a salty tongue in his mouth. With a hand on his cheek and the other close to his dick, the painter embraced the girl's warmth with a hug.

"What happened? Did I do something?" asked Priya.

"Oh no no. I just wanted a hug," said Priyesh.

"Cool," said Priya. "I am in the six-bed dorm. See you soon!"

"Done," Priyesh said, still shaking—petrified of the hand.

XI

By the Beach

The day you look forward to eventually arrives. Sooner or later, everyone faces what they need to. But exceptions may be there. Some people might get by without answering for the mess they put others in.

"Time just flew by fast, didn't it? Like a rabid dog, you sought to be put down. But what now? What are you left with?" texted Anvi.

Priya left a day ago. The hostel was nearly closing down. One more day, and an entire building where he met so many people would become alien.

The phone vibrated. It was Mary.

"Hey Priyesh! Why don't we hang out today? There is this architecture museum I want to go to. Meet me at this location I'm sending, and maybe we can try this wine I got," Mary said.

"Sure," Priyesh retorted, dropping all the thoughts, running down the stairs towards his rented two-wheeler.

In front of the cafe, he could see Kunal talking to someone.

"He drew the sketch on the table," Kunal said, pointing to Priyesh, asking him to come closer.

"Hi, I'm Guru. I must say that you've got mad skills," the unknown said.

"Thanks!" Priyesh replied. "So, what do you do?"

"I travel and have ventures here and there," said Guru.

"So, what are you working on now?" Priyesh asked.

"Myself," said Guru.

"Meaning?" Priyesh wondered. "Wait a second, I think I heard my phone. It's my ex. She keeps texting me."

"But I didn't hear anything," said Guru.

"Really? I swear I heard it," said Priyesh. "Strange."

"It is fine; it happens with me too," said Guru.

"You should meet my ex. She is such an asshole," said Priyesh.

"Just like a dog, your tail keeps coming back to blaming her," Guru said. "I do understand."

"Oh, the coffee's here," interrupted Kunal.

"Thank you, sir," said Guru.

"So, where are you going?" asked Kunal.

"I'm going to meet with Miss Mary," said Priyesh. "We have something planned today."

"Oh, that is nice," said Kunal.

"Your excitement shows that this girl means something to you," said Guru.

"Oh yeah. I kind of like her, and she's quite cool," said Priyesh.

"Aren't they all?" Guru said, adding, "People are excellent at disappointing you. Once the excitement fades, you'll be left stranded, questioning every decision you've ever made."

"But that is the source of my art, I believe," said the painter. "A colorless life, for art fails to blossom in comfort."

"Woah!" exclaimed Kunal. "Damn!"

"Okay, I'm getting late now. Will see you guys soon," said Priyesh.

"This motherfucker is weird," said Priyesh, while staring at Guru from afar.

***

"Hey," Mary shouted, hugging Priyesh. "Another day in fuckin' paradise!"

The museum stood in front of the two. It was actually four floors of factual data on different types of Goan and Portuguese architecture.

The lady at the reception collected the entry fee. The shoes were to be removed. The procedure was pretty quick and straightforward.

Priyesh roamed around the first floor, then the second, then the third, and finally he stood atop the building—the fifth floor that had a dated piece of architecture hidden from usual eyes.

This strange miniscule building had a door, about the height of the painter, and he entered it. He could hear someone faintly calling his name out.

A foul odor had found its way into the structure, and it was completely dark inside. The door using which Priyesh had entered was no longer there.

The painter stood atop a large black floor. He jumped up and down to break out of the structure. But there was no upper limit of the structure, all of a sudden.

Confusion and panic set in. Priyesh started walking haphazardly, looking for an exit. A few minutes into the search, he began running.

The painter ran towards a destination unknown—looking for an exit that did not exist until it did—suddenly a spotlight dropped on Priyesh.

The floor could be seen—a similar painting. He was walking on the first painting he ever made on a birthday cake cardboard.

People were laughing at him. A canvas stood in front of him. A paintbrush in his hand and yet no vision, only darkness.

"Was the table sketch the best you could do?" said a man, throwing a bottle from the crowd as another spotlight revealed the table next to Priyesh.

"Wait," Priyesh said, trying his best to make a beautiful final painting. He made a girl lost in a dreamy world; a boy lost beneath humongous leaves that hid his face—only to reveal large blue eyes; and he also made an old man, wearing a turban with black eyes and saffron clothing, who was skateboarding.

"Boo!" said the crowd. "This isn't enough. You are filthy. Unworthy! Go back! Fuck off."

Dejected, the painter turned away from the crowd, only to find a hand in front of him.

Priyesh froze once again. His eyes did not move. His tongue was dead. The hand grabbed the painter by the neck, choking him as darkness once again clouded his vision.

***

"It seems like this place has been abandoned for quite a while," Priyesh said.

He found a dark green bench with rusted parts and broken sides and sat down, looking at the skies, at flocks of birds soaring through the skies, making weird patterns as they claimed their territory.

"Is one of you the bird I set free? I can't really differentiate—you all just seem shadowy to me," Priyesh thought.

The painter turned his focus to the multiple tree branches above him. One branch had dark green leaves, the other had light green, and some were rotten, disease-struck leaves.

An hour passed with Priyesh looking at those tree leaves.

"Hey! I have been looking for you! Where have you been?" Mary asked, finally ending her half-hour search for Priyesh. "What are you doing, sitting all alone?"

"Nothing. I just came down after spending some time on the fifth floor. Found this spot, and moments ago I was wondering if the trees differentiated on the basis of color," Priyesh said.

"Oh Jesus! You and your thinking will surely land you nowhere. I have been searching all over for you. I am leaving tomorrow!" said Mary.

"Well, what's next?" Priyesh asked?

"There is a beach nearby. We can go there," said Mary.

Priyesh agreed, and the duo ended up in a cafe close to the beach.

***

"I wanted to ask something. How much investment, including the land cost, have you made in this cafe?" Mary asked the owner.

"Around 50 lakh INR," said the owner.

"What is a lakh, and how much is it in euros?" Mary asked Priyesh, who wasn't speaking much.

"It is around 54,000 euros," Priyesh said.

"That is not much, is it?" Mary said. "I could earn that in like a few months."

The owner got a little embarrassed.

"Well, thank you!" said Mary and turned to Priyesh. "I was telling you about the time I was shamed for not developing early."

"Yeah. It is all fun and nice," Priyesh said.

"Are you upset?" Mary asked.

"No!" Priyesh added.

"You know, we have great chemistry, but sometimes, if two friends hook up, the friendship just gets ruined," Mary said.

"Well, I don't even care much about sex. I get it when I want it, and right now, I'm not in the mindset to get physical with someone," Priyesh replied.

"You're a cool guy," said Mary. "The Portuguese guy—look at him, he is so gorgeous!"

Priyesh saw Mary's boyfriend—possibly the most handsome man he ever saw.

"You're not speaking much. C'mon, I'm leaving tomorrow. You are going to be silent the whole time?" Mary asked. "Come meet me in the morning before I leave; I'll let you taste the wine."

Priyesh agreed again, returning to the hostel.

***

The second-to-last day arrived with one more day to go.

With droopy eyes and a large beard, Priyesh looked at himself in the mirror in the bathroom, wondering if this was it.

"You haven't decided, have you?" he asked himself. "You're a coward."

Priyesh splashed water on his face, getting ready for his final meeting with Mary.

After the bathroom, he checked his phone for messages. There were none. The older texts are gone—just like that.

"What?!" Priyesh reacted.

He ran downstairs to check on his sketch—still unsure if that is the last artwork he wanted.

Most of the staff and the guests had already gone, and the building was almost empty.

Priyesh left to meet Mary.

***

He landed in the mermaid's sanctuary, where Miss Mary sang a tune, which became one with the sound of the waves coming from the nearby beach.

The trees hid the ruthless sun, and the narrow paths led to a short gate where a dusky, well-built man was watering his plants.

Two dogs ran towards the gates when they realized that a stranger had entered, barking at the top of their lungs.

The dusky man, also wearing a hat and a sleeveless shirt, came close to the gate, saying, "Hi there! It seems you're lost. Where do you seek to go?"

"Do you happen to know a German named Mary?" asked Priyesh.

"Oh yes. Marilyn. I'll take you to her," said the man as Priyesh started following him.

"So, is this all your property?" the painter asked.

"Yes," said the man. "I was fortunate enough that my father and his father bought all this land and left me with it."

Seconds later, Priyesh saw Mary seated in front of her door with her laptop, wearing a pink top and a white skirt.

"Good morning! You're on time. I have it all planned. First, we'll taste this wine, then we'll go to the beach and have mango lassi."

"It is early in the morning," said Priyesh.

"Did not listen," she said, running inside and bringing out two glasses, pouring wine into them.

"Ew!" the painter said. "This just tastes sour. Why would anyone drink this?"

Mary burst into laughter while Priyesh looked at a painting on the wall that read, "Everything has its beauty, but not everyone chooses to see it."

"Hey! Mr. Thinker, let's go to the beach," said Mary.

The duo went towards the beach, about two minutes of a pleasant walk away.

A tapered path where tourists sunbathed in the leftmost corner of Anjuna Beach—not many people came there.

"I wanted to show you this," Mary said, asking Priyesh to continue following her.

The narrow lanes adjacent to the beach finally ended, unveiling an enormous chunk of land with mangrove trees and huge, slippery rocks all around.

"Did you see that old couple a few minutes ago?" Mary asked.

"Yes, I did!" Priyesh replied.

"I can swear that when I'm 60, I will look exactly like the lady," said Mary.

"I don't remember how she looked," Priyesh said.

"Well, you missed it," Mary added.

"I'm going to have a smoke. See you in a bit," said the painter while walking towards a cluster of rocks, hopping from one to another.

Finally, he sat still on the cornermost rock, taking out his cigarette and smoking it.

A tall and very thin man came towards Priyesh, asking for a lighter to light up his cigarette.

"Here you go," said the painter.

The man took out his cigarette, which was actually marijuana.

"Man, I swear I've seen you somewhere. Were you in the hostel in Arpora?" questioned Priyesh.

"Dude, there are hundreds of hostels in Goa, maybe even more. You could've seen a lookalike, maybe? Also, I'm a local. Why would I stay in hostels?" the man explained.

"Contradictory," wondered Priyesh.

If your time in this city was printed on sheets,
The ink would dry up;
The stories—deeper than a cup.

Your fault?
You don't want to leave;
Don't want to go away,
But travelers never stay.

The narrow roads, the heat, the breezy nights,
It's beautiful to experience the blinding lights.

If you throw your fist in the air,
At the thought of leaving—
It wouldn't be fair.

You got what you came here for,
There's no point in searching for more.
You're a whore:
Outgrowing beds that you used to sleep—
Leaving behind shattered pieces of a broken life.

A liar, a thief, a cheater,
But, above all,
What you live is not just life—
It's art; it's theater.

XII
Creator's Creative Hand

"Thank you for the lighter. I will see you in a bit," said the thin man.

Mary called out to Priyesh, "Hey! Come back! I have something for you."

"See you later," Priyesh told the man, leaving for Mary.

He ran towards the German, stopping right beside her, "Yes, Miss Mary!"

Mary laughed out loud. "You're cute! Artists such as yourself—first-world-country problems in third-world countries—are not able to price your own art, no matter how much you try."

"And where did you hear this?" Priyesh asked.

"C'mon, give me some credit. I'm much older than you. I know about stuff," said Mary.

"Cool," said Priyesh.

"Okay. We have to go further. Follow me," said Mary.

"Let's go then," Priyesh said.

The duo went down a narrow strip of land, slightly submerged under water amid humongous rocks. Once the path ended, the two saw a huge tree.

A little further down the path, and there were massive rocks facing the sea and open skies—a corner of the beach rarely visited by anyone anymore.

"Isn't it like a beach inside a beach?" Priyesh said.

"This is like a mini beach," laughed Mary. "Look at that tree. And the rocks!"

"Wow," said Priyesh. "Haven't seen anything like this in forever!"

"C'mon, follow me," said Mary, jumping from one rock to another, unaware that they were slippery, possibly due to algae buildup.

"You go, I will follow," said Priyesh, drawing a palm tree using his index finger in the sand.

A thud was heard. The German fell hard, her lower back and hips getting smashed against rocks.

"Oh shit! Are you okay? Mary!" shouted Priyesh from afar and ran towards the German.

"Don't!" Mary said while her head went numb, her vision blank from pain.

Priyesh panicked and sped up, jumping from one rock to another. The painter lost balance.

His speed was more, weight was more, and balance was less—the painter fell into the sea, his head hitting a rock. The water pulled him towards the bottom.

The situation was still salvageable, if only Mary could call for help and Priyesh could climb a few rocks, distancing himself from the sea.

The painter used his right hand to grab on to a sharp rock, but his left hand wouldn't move. It wasn't stuck, but it just won't move.

He looked close and saw another hand holding his left one, forcing him towards the water.

The tug-of-war only lasted a few seconds as a strong wave emerged, dragging the painter away in seconds.

Mary screamed for help as, within a few minutes, a crowd gathered.

Priyesh waved his legs around inside the water, his nose and eyes burning, his head aching as he saw his own blood mixing with ocean water.

He wanted to push his body up and try to give some kind of signal to others, but he wasn't able to use the left arm. Priyesh used both his legs to reduce the scarred hand's grip on his arm—the grip only got stronger.

Priyesh struggled; the hand haunting him did not let go. Water started entering through his nose—he couldn't even shed a tear.

***

"When you were young, you were fair like cotton balls. Your mother told me that people used to look at you like you were a miracle," said the tall and thin man. "Yet she never loved you enough to pay for swimming lessons, did she?"

"She paid. I used to skip them," Priyesh said.

"The last time you visited the old woman, she had two front teeth missing. She was not happy with the way her son's life turned out," said the man. "Do you miss her? At this moment?"

"Nope," said the painter. "Maybe a little. But I would say I miss many people more than I miss my mother."

"Silence and work—your father was focused on these two—there is nothing more to life than these two thrown into a blender and drinking that shit every morning," the thin man narrated.

"I don't miss him either," said Priyesh.

"Then who?" the man asked. "Anvi?"

"The first time I met Anvi was outside an elevator of a cafe. She was possibly attending a party, drinking shots like crazy, smoking as much as she could, and finally, in an attempt to find the washroom, ended up near the lift," the painter narrated.

"The lift opened, and there Anvi was, looking for a place to pee. She asked me about the washroom, and I told her. She stumbled here and there. I helped the drunkard, and while she possibly vomited in a commode, I waited for her outside. Once back, I asked if I could drop her home," Priyesh said.

"Then what?" asked the man.

"She said she didn't want to go home because of her family shit. Then I took her to my apartment. Gave her my bed, and she didn't leave for a few years. 'It is your expectations from the viewers. You're wondering if people look at your paintings and feel the same way you do when looking at yours or other artists' paintings. They may or may not,' she told me. But I wasn't selling any, and my heart broke—despite efforts, I had no money," said Priyesh.

"Okay, well, fuck everything else. Tell me—do you like your final artwork?" the man questioned.

"What? The sketch on the table?" asked Priyesh. "Didn't even get to complete it, or even capture a photo, man."

"Ah, no. Not the sketch. The palm tree, in the sand. Do you like it?" the man asked.

"I can live with it," said Priyesh.

"Except, you're not," the man told the painter—both giggling at just a painter's life.

"What about the hand?" asked Priyesh.

"Here," said the man, extending his scarred hand. "The Creator's Creative Hand."

"What was the point?" asked the painter.
"Of?" asked the man.
"Everything," said Priyesh.
"The sea will find its way to you—to soak you and become one with you. On the last day in paradise, you will find that you wanted to be drenched, that you would've given everything to accept the thoughts you've conjured in your heart and drawn in the sand," said the tall, thin man.

Loss:
A term borned from our flaws.
The mistakes you made, pushing people far,
In search of the moon, all you could see was a star.

Spent days overthinking,
Only to realize you weren't actually thinking—
Just pondering the same emotion over and over again, sinking.

Life was too short to hold grudges,
You claimed to stand above all the judges.
Diving headfirst into situations—
You had no control over was a trait,
The consequences—nothing is up to fate.

Relationships you should mend, people you can forgive,
But you don't want to anymore—
You don't have anymore to give,
An empty vessel, I will take you ashore.

A man stared at me for being rude,
I burned his heart—
I'm not a bitter person,

But what grinds my gears?
People don't have open minds, but are all ears.

The Creator's Creative Hand,
The master of colors, the demon inside art:
You kept asking for me—
Here I am, right next to where you stand.

* 9 7 9 8 8 9 5 1 9 4 1 0 2 *